MICHELLE

Michelle has a great idea! She's going to put on a show with her friends and sell tickets to help benefit a worthy San Francisco charity. All her friends are psyched to be in the show and help out the cause. And Michelle is totally ready to write the show, direct it, and star in it.

STEPHANIE

But Stephanie has another idea. She's run into a friend, Heather "Peace" Smith, who recently appeared on the popular teen show *Summer's Cove*. Peace is a star! If Stephanie can get her to be in the show, it will be big, huge, tremendously popular!

There's just one problem. When Peace says she'll be in the show, Stephanie totally takes over, rearranging everything Michelle has planned.

Can two sisters learn to compromise and work together? Or will the show *not* go on?

FULL HOUSE™: SISTERS books

Two on the Town
One Boss Too Many
And the Winner Is . . .
How to Hide a Horse
Problems in Paradise
Will You Be My Valentine?
Let's Put On a Show
Baby-sitters & Company
  (coming soon)

Available from MINSTREL Books

For orders other than by individual consumers, Pocket Books grants a discount on the purchase of **10 or more** copies of single titles for special markets or premium use. For further details, please write to the Vice President of Special Markets, Pocket Books, 1230 Avenue of the Americas, 9th Floor, New York, NY 10020-1586.

For information on how individual consumers can place orders, please write to Mail Order Department, Simon & Schuster Inc., 100 Front Street, Riverside, NJ 08075.

FULL HOUSE™

Sisters

Let's Put On a Show

ELIZABETH WINFREY

A Parachute Press Book

Published by POCKET BOOKS
New York   London   Toronto   Sydney   Singapore

The sale of this book without its cover is unauthorized. If you purchased this book without a cover, you should be aware that it was reported to the publisher as "unsold and destroyed." Neither the author nor the publisher has received payment for the sale of this "stripped book."

This book is a work of fiction. Names, characters, places and incidents are products of the author's imagination or are used fictitiously. Any resemblance to actual events or locales or persons living or dead is entirely coincidental.

A MINSTREL PAPERBACK *Original*

 A Minstrel Book published by
POCKET BOOKS, a division of Simon & Schuster Inc.
1230 Avenue of the Americas, New York, NY 10020

A PARACHUTE PRESS BOOK

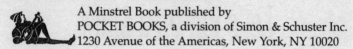 Copyright © and ™ 2000 by Warner Bros.

FULL HOUSE, characters, names and all related indicia are trademarks of Warner Bros. © 2000.

All rights reserved, including the right to reproduce this book or portions thereof in any form whatsoever. For information address Pocket Books, 1230 Avenue of the Americas, New York, NY 10020

ISBN: 0-671-04088-X

First Minstrel Books printing March 2000

10 9 8 7 6 5 4 3 2 1

A MINSTREL BOOK and colophon are registered trademarks of Simon & Schuster Inc.

Printed in the U.S.A.

Chapter
1

Stephanie Tanner flung open the front door of the Tanners' three-story San Francisco town house. "Dad, where are you?" she cried. "I've got something awesome to show you!"

"In the living room, Steph," Danny Tanner called back. "Come on in. You're just in time for one of Michelle's mini-recitals."

Stephanie tried not to groan when she headed into the living room and saw her little sister standing on the piece of plywood that she used to practice her tap routines.

Usually Stephanie was happy to watch Michelle do one of her numbers. After all, part of the job of being a big sister included cheer-

1

ing on and coaching your little sister when she needed you.

If she didn't tell her dad her immense news right now she was sure she was going to burst!

"This will only take a second," Stephanie promised as she plopped down on the sofa next to her father. "I just have to show you—"

"Okay, Dad, I'm ready," Michelle interrupted. She flipped her blond ponytail over a shoulder and hit a pose—one hand on her hip, the other in a snappy salute. "Hit the music!"

Danny leaned across the coffee table and pressed Play on the tape recorder. The song "I'm a Yankee Doodle Dandy" started blaring and Michelle began tapping.

Stephanie reached into her backpack and yanked out the newest issue of *Daisy*, her favorite teen magazine. It fell open to the exact page she wanted to show her dad.

"Look," she whispered. She nudged her father's arm with the magazine.

"Wait until she's through," Danny whispered back. He kept his eyes locked on Michelle.

Stephanie sighed. As if they both hadn't

seen her do the "Yankee Doodle Dandy" number a zillion times.

Oh, well, Stephanie thought. *If I'm going to have to watch this for the zillion and first time, I may as well give Michelle some tips.*

After all, Stephanie figured, she had been taking dance lessons for four more years than Michelle had. She learned a lot of things in those four years that she could teach her little sister.

She studied Michelle as she did the first combination. Step. Step. Shuffle. Kick.

"Keep your left leg straight when you do that kick, Michelle," Stephanie instructed.

Michelle frowned as she concentrated. She did another kick.

Her leg was straighter, but something still wasn't right.

"Snap your leg out from the knee, Michelle," Stephanie told her. "And point your toes. That will give you a perfect line. And your kick will look cleaner."

Michelle's frown deepened. She did another kick.

Perfect, but Michelle was frowning so deeply, it looked as if she was totally angry!

3

"And smile, Michelle!" Stephanie cried. "Smile! If people are looking at your face, your bad kicks won't be so noticeable."

Michelle stopped tapping. She snapped off the tape recorder and glared at Stephanie.

"Why did you stop?" Danny asked. "What's wrong? You were doing great!"

"Not according to Stephanie," Michelle complained.

"You were doing fine. I was just trying to help you do better," Stephanie protested. "Sometimes it's hard to know if you're doing the moves right if there's no one watching and telling you. I bet you didn't even realize you had that scowl on your face."

"Oh, I realized it. It doesn't exactly make me feel like smiling when *someone* is yelling at me every five seconds," Michelle shot back, her face bright red.

Whoa! She's majorly angry, Stephanie realized.

"Now, wait a minute," Danny started to say.

"Michelle, don't be so sensitive," she said. "I just want you to be the best you can be. Come on. Start again."

Stephanie pressed Rewind on the tape player.

4

Michelle stabbed the Stop button.

Whoa! Stephanie thought. *That was totally rude!*

Stephanie stared at her sister. Didn't Michelle get it? Stephanie was just trying to help.

"Uhhh—girls—" Danny began.

"Aunt Becky said I was great when I did the dance for her," Michelle interrupted. She planted her hands on her hips. "So did Uncle Jesse. And Joey. And you heard Dad. He just said I was great, too!"

"Don't forget the twins," Stephanie muttered.

She didn't know anyone who had as many people living in a house as she did. Her mom died when she was a little kid. After that Danny asked his best friend, Joey Gladstone, and his brother-in-law, Jesse Katzopolis, to move in to help take care of Stephanie, Michelle, and their older sister, D.J. Then Uncle Jesse married Aunt Becky, and the two of them had twin boys, Nicky and Alex. That made nine people in a very full house.

"That's right! The twins loved it, too," Michelle shot back. "They made me do it three times."

And four-year-olds know so *much about tap dancing*, Stephanie thought. *Next she's going to tell me that Comet gave her a standing ovation.*

Their big golden retriever *did* start barking whenever Michelle started tapping. But Stephanie suspected it was because he didn't like the noise.

"Michelle, I think you did a great job, too," Stephanie said, trying super hard to sound calm and reasonable. "But I think there are a couple of ways you could be even *more* fantastic. Like, you—"

"I don't want to hear it!" Michelle exclaimed. "You're always telling me what to do. 'Michelle, raisins would be much better in the pancakes than marshmallows.' 'Michelle, that color pink makes your face look kind of green.' 'Michelle, don't you think you should wear your shoes instead of your sneakers? Blah, blah, blah, blah, BLAH!' "

Michelle's voice got higher and louder with every *blah.*

Stephanie told herself to stay cool. She had to. It was her job as a big sister. But how could she? Michelle was being totally ridiculous!

Was Stephanie supposed to let Michelle go

off to school with a face as green as a frog's? Or let her destroy their dad's favorite pan with sticky marshmallows? Or let her walk into a fancy restaurant wearing sneakers?

"Now, wait a minute, girls," Danny started again.

"If you don't want my help—fine!" Stephanie yelled over him. "See what a mess you make of everything on your own."

"I won't make a mess!" Michelle shouted. "You think I don't know anything, but I do and I don't need you to—"

"Okay, that's enough from both of you!" Danny interrupted.

"I was just trying to be a good big sister," Stephanie tried to explain. "It's part of my job to give advice and—"

Michelle didn't let her finish. "Well, it's not your job anymore," she cried. "Stephanie—you are no longer my big sister. You're fired!"

MICHELLE

Chapter
2

Stephanie blinked. "You're firing me as your sister?" she demanded. Her blue eyes blazed with anger. "You can't do that!"

"I can, and I just did!" Michelle answered. She realized she was breathing fast and that her face felt really warm.

She had never felt so mad at her sister in her whole life! Who did Stephanie think she was, anyway? Sometimes it seemed as if she never even bothered to talk to Michelle unless she wanted to tell her what to do.

"I said, that's enough!" Danny exclaimed. He pushed himself up from the sofa and stood in front of the two girls.

8

"Have a seat," he told Michelle. "Now."

Michelle flopped down on the couch. She positioned herself as far away from Stephanie as she could. Her father pulled up a chair and sat facing them. He looked from Michelle to Stephanie and back. Then he cleared his throat.

Oh, great, Michelle thought. *He's about to give us a huge big lecture.*

"Sorry, Michelle. You can't just fire Stephanie," he began. "You two are going to be sisters for your whole lives. It's one of the most important relationships—"

"Oh, there you are, Danny!" Aunt Becky hurried into the living room. "I thought before dinner we could watch the video of the little girl we're interviewing tomorrow—"

She stopped short when she saw the serious expressions on everyone's faces. "Oh. Obviously I'm interrupting something."

"That's okay," Michelle said quickly.

Aunt Becky shot a questioning look at Danny.

"You know what? It really is okay," he answered. "In fact, I think it would be good for all of us to see this video."

9

"Why? What's on it?" Stephanie asked. Michelle could tell that she was eager to get their dad on another subject, too. "What did the girl do to get interviewed on your show?"

Danny and Aunt Becky co-hosted a local morning TV show called *Wake Up, San Francisco!* They often came home with interesting stories about people and places in the city.

"The little girl's name is Samantha O'Reilly," Danny explained. "She has a disease that is affecting her nervous system. There is a new surgical procedure that might be able to help her, but it's very expensive."

"She has to have an operation?" Michelle asked. Her father nodded.

Michelle bit her lip. She couldn't imagine going to the hospital and having an operation. Poor Samantha!

"We're going to ask our viewers to help Samantha. We're hoping to raise at least part of the money she needs to have her surgery," Aunt Becky added. She popped the video in the VCR, and a second later the tape began to play.

A girl in a pink leotard stood in front of a barre in a dance studio. She began doing pliés—bending her knees outward—the same exercise Michelle used to warm up at her dance lessons. Her red hair was pulled back in a ponytail.

I always pull my hair into a ponytail for dance class, too, Michelle thought. For some reason, a yucky feeling crept into her stomach.

"Is that Samantha?" Michelle whispered. "She looks like she's the same age as I am."

"Just a little younger," Danny answered. "She's eight."

"She doesn't look sick," Stephanie added.

"I think this part was taken in the very early stages of the disease," Aunt Becky said gently.

A few moments later the TV screen went blank. Then a new image appeared—Samantha in a wheelchair. The spokes of the wheels had glittery pink and blue ribbons woven through them.

"I like those," Michelle said, pointing to the TV.

"Samantha's mom put the ribbons there. Those are her favorite colors," Aunt Becky added.

Michelle stared at the television. "Her favorite colors are the same as mine," she whis-

11

pered. She loved pink and blue more than any other color combination.

She leaned forward and listened hard as Samantha began to speak. "In the morning my mom helps me get dressed," Samantha explained to someone standing off camera. "Then she brushes my hair because I can't hold the brush very well." Her hands gave an awkward twist in her lap.

"My brother did my hair for me once," she added. "But only once. Brothers do not understand the hair thing. I mean, he couldn't even make a braid."

"Hey!" a guy called from off camera. "It wasn't that bad."

Samantha laughed. "He pushes my chair really fast, though. So I guess I'll keep him. Although sometimes I think it would be nice to have a sister, too."

Stephanie reached over and took Michelle's hand. Michelle didn't pull away. Suddenly she didn't feel like being as far away from Stephanie as possible. Not anymore.

"After that, my dad usually helps me eat breakfast. I'm not great at holding a fork, either," Samantha continued.

"I help, too, sometimes," the same guy called from out of camera range.

"That's true," Samantha said. "My brother does help me eat. But he spills almost as much on me as he usually does on himself."

"Hey!" A Nerf ball flew out from the left of the screen and bopped Samantha on the head.

Samantha laughed again. So did Michelle and Stephanie.

"She's so cool. I mean, she can still laugh at stuff," Stephanie said. She paused.

"The operation will fix her, right?" she asked Danny.

"The doctors hope so," he answered. "And we're going to do everything we can to get her the money for her hospital stay."

"It's not so bad going to school in a wheel-chair," Samantha started saying. "At least, not as bad as you would figure."

"Shhh!" Michelle shushed her family. She didn't want to miss even one of Samantha's words.

She tried to imagine how difficult it would be to go to *her* school in a wheelchair. Recess would be the hardest. She wondered what Samantha did while the other kids were running around on the playground. But Samantha didn't say anything about that part of her day.

She skipped to a description of all the doctors she'd seen in the past few months. She had a funny story about almost all of them.

I bet it wasn't that funny when she was actually in all those doctors' offices, though, Michelle thought.

The screen went blank for another few seconds, and then some kind of family dinner came on the screen. Michelle spotted a large turkey in the center of the table. That must be Thanksgiving, she decided.

"I'm thankful that Dad missed my skateboard when he pulled into the driveway yesterday, and I'm thankful that Ms. Hahn got sick so the spelling test was canceled," the boy next to Samantha said.

"That must be her brother," Stephanie whispered.

Michelle nodded. He had the same red hair as Samantha. Except a cap was turned sideways on top of it. Michelle thought he definitely didn't look like someone who would know how to make a braid.

"Is that enough?" the boy asked the older woman at the head of the table.

"That's enough," the woman—Michelle figured it was Samantha's mother—answered. "Your turn, Sammi."

Samantha closed her eyes for a minute. Her forehead got all crinkly. It looked like she was thinking hard. "I guess I'm just thankful for my family," she said. She grinned at her brother. "Even you, Steve."

The screen went blank again, and this time it stayed blank. Michelle just stared at it a second, feeling totally sad.

Danny turned around so he was facing Michelle and Stephanie again. "I think Samantha made my point better than I could," he said. "Family is the most important thing any of us have. Not only when we're sick or in trouble, but always."

"We're lucky," Aunt Becky put in as she rewound the video. "We have a large family. And we all should appreciate one another."

Stephanie gave Michelle's hand a squeeze. "So am I rehired as your sister?" she asked.

Michelle smiled. "Definitely," she answered.

"Okay, so let's see that routine again," Stephanie said.

Michelle groaned. "Steph, I promise you I'll never fire you again. But could you do me one favor?"

"Of course," Stephanie answered. "Anything."

"Please, please don't watch me do my tap dance again," Michelle begged. "Ever."

"You got it," Stephanie said.

"And don't tell me what I should put in my pancakes," Michelle added.

"No problem," Stephanie said.

"And don't tell me what color shirt to wear," Michelle told her.

"Come on, Michelle," Stephanie protested. "I'm your big sister. You have to let me be a little bossy."

Michelle thought it over. Samantha would probably take any kind of sister—even a bossy one.

"Okay," Michelle said. "You can be a little bossy. But just a teeny, tiny, little bit."

"You can count on me, Michelle," Stephanie pledged. "I promise I won't ever boss you around again."

MICHELLE

Chapter
3

I wonder if Samantha O'Reilly likes turkey casserole, Michelle thought. Her dad slid a spoonful of one of his special dishes onto her plate.

Practically every other minute since she'd seen the video, Michelle found herself thinking of Samantha. She couldn't stop—even now, at dinner. Her entire family was gathered around the kitchen table and Michelle couldn't keep the sick girl out of her head.

"You said you had something to show me earlier, Steph." Danny slid some casserole onto Stephanie's plate. "What was it?" he asked.

Stephanie jumped up from the table. "Oh! I

totally forgot!" she exclaimed. "You've all got to see this." She raced out of the room. A few seconds later she sped back in clutching a copy of *Daisy* magazine.

I wonder if Samantha reads Daisy, Michelle thought.

"Guess who this is?" Stephanie held up a picture of a beautiful teenage girl. She was slim and graceful-looking, with long, dark hair and green eyes. She wore a lime-green dress with a funky silver zipper down the front.

"Isn't she the girl who was in that movie-of-the-week on TV the other night?" Aunt Becky asked.

"She's in some styling gel commercial, too, isn't she?" Uncle Jesse added.

"You would know, Mr. Perfect Hair," Joey teased him.

"Yes and yes," Stephanie answered. "But that's not what's amazing." She waved the picture in front of Danny's face. "Doesn't she look familiar?"

Danny studied the picture, frowning.

"Think about that Muppet movie you took me and my friends to," Stephanie hinted. "Think about my first slumber party."

18

"Hey! That's Heather Smith!" Danny burst out. He took the magazine from Stephanie to study the picture more closely.

"She changed her name to Peace, but, yeah. It's Heather," Stephanie explained. "We were in the first grade together," she told the rest of the table.

"Cool! You know a celebrity!" Michelle exclaimed.

"I think I remember her," D.J. said. "She looks totally different without those glasses she used to wear."

"She's going to be signing autographs at the mall tomorrow," Stephanie announced. "I'm thinking of going and saying hi."

"You should," Uncle Jesse told her.

"Yeah, maybe you can strike up a friendship again. Then you'll be hanging out with a *star!*" Joey whipped a pair of sunglasses out of his pocket. He put them on, then turned up his collar. He nodded in a totally cool way to everyone at the table.

"Except she might not remember me," Stephanie said. "And that would be pretty humiliating."

"Of course she'll remember you," Michelle

insisted. "I remember everyone in my first-grade class."

Stephanie frowned at Peace's photo. "I don't know. Peace has really changed a lot," she muttered.

"Can I see?" Michelle asked Stephanie. Her sister handed over the magazine, and Michelle studied the picture. It was hard to believe Peace Smith was the same age as Stephanie. She looked more like D.J.'s age. Or at least old enough to be a senior in high school.

Also she was so pretty, she could practically be Miss America. Michelle couldn't believe Stephanie actually knew someone that beautiful.

I wonder if Samantha likes Peace Smith, Michelle thought.

"I want to see *peas* Smith, too," Nicky piped up.

"Peace, not peas," Stephanie corrected him. She wiped off his sticky hands with a napkin. "Hey, Nicky. Next time try eating your casserole with your spoon. It will be a lot less messy."

Michelle felt a little smile tug at her lips.

Good, she thought. *Let Stephanie get all her bossiness out on the twins. They're little. They still need someone to tell them what to do.*

As she started to hand the magazine back to her sister an article caught her eye.

The headline read: "Helping Hands Reach Out."

Michelle scanned the first several paragraphs of the article. Her heart began to pound. The story was about a boy in Seattle named Tim Hellerman.

Tim and his friends wanted to help the homeless kids in their city, so they all got together and put on a talent show. They gave all the money they made to a local soup kitchen.

Stephanie gave the magazine a gentle tug, and Michelle let go. She'd read enough—enough to get an amazing idea!

Michelle shoveled down the rest of her casserole. She ate so fast, she hardly tasted it. Then she drained her glass of milk.

"Can I be excused?" she blurted out. "I have something important to do. Something really, really important."

Her father smiled at her. "Well, if it's really, really important, then go ahead."

"Thanks!" Michelle bolted out of the dining room and raced up to the bedroom she shared with Stephanie.

First she needed a sheet of stationery. She wanted to use her very best—the paper with the pink-and-blue polka-dot border that Stephanie had given her for her last birthday.

Michelle found the box in the bottom drawer of her desk. Only one piece left. She'd have to be careful not to make any mistakes.

She sat down and pulled a pink felt-tip pen out of the cup in front of her. She took off the cap, thought for a minute, then started to write.

Dear Samantha,

She decided to say Samantha and not Sammi, because she figured maybe Samantha's mother was the only one who used her nickname.

Now what?

Michelle thought so long, her pen started to dry up. She dunked it quickly in the cup of water next to her bed. *Better remember not to drink that water,* she thought. Then she started to write again.

Let's Put On a Show

You don't know me, but my dad, Danny Tanner, brought a videotape of you home. He did it to get ready for his interview with you. I watched it, too. I hope that's okay.

I noticed that you like pink and blue. Those are my favorite colors, too, as you can see from this paper. I bet there are lots of things we both like.

My dad and my aunt Becky are going to ask the people who watch their show to send in money so you can get the operation you need. I bet that everyone will send tons of money. But my friends and I want to help, too.

Michelle hadn't actually talked to her friends yet, but she was sure they *would* want to help when they heard all about Samantha.

She flipped over the sheet of paper and continued the letter.

We're going to put on a talent show and sell tickets. Then we'll send all the money we make to you. So don't worry. You're absolutely, positively going to be

able to get the operation, and you are
going to get one hundred percent better. I
just know it.

She had a little more space left. She tapped
the top of her pen against her lips, trying to
figure out the perfect way to close her letter.

She thought about telling Samantha that
she'd send her an invitation to the show.

Michelle wasn't sure that Samantha would
be feeling well enough to come, though.

I know! Michelle thought. She started to
write again.

We'll make a video for you so you and
your family can see the show.
Bye for now.

Love, Michelle (Tanner)

She carefully folded the sheet of paper and
stuck it in a pink-and-blue polka-dotted envelope. She would ask her father to give it to
Samantha when he saw her.

Now that she had decided to put on a show
for Samantha, it was time to start a list of
everything she would need. She ripped a

piece of paper out of her binder and started to write again.

Tickets, definitely. Posters, yup. Plus a place to put on the show. Oh, and, of course, *acts*. Michelle was determined to think up a bunch of amazing acts that people would want to see.

There were still lots of things Michelle couldn't decide about. Like should they try to serve refreshments? Where were they going to get costumes? How much should they charge people to see the show? Who would take tickets at the door?

More and more questions crowded into Michelle's brain.

Whoa. Maybe her amazing idea wasn't so amazing after all. Maybe this show was too much for her to handle.

She wouldn't have to do it all by herself, she reminded herself. Her best friends, Cassie Wilkins and Mandy Metz, would definitely help, and she bet a lot of their other friends would, too.

If those kids in Seattle can do it, we can do it, she told herself. *This is going to be great! We are totally going to help Samantha get better!*

Chapter
4

Stephanie ladled pancake batter onto the hot skillet. *I love Saturday mornings,* she thought.

One of the reasons she loved them was that she had plenty of time to make her specialty—pancakes—for whoever got up on time.

"The perfect pancake," Stephanie commented as she flipped the circle of bubbling batter.

"Yum!" Michelle exclaimed. She walked into the kitchen and peered into the pan Stephanie was using. "Is there enough batter for me?"

"Of course," Stephanie answered. "I made enough to feed the whole neighborhood." She slid a spatula under the pancake and flipped it onto a plate.

"Oh, and here." Stephanie pulled a bag of mini-marshmallows out of the cupboard. "I thought you might want to put these on." She grinned at her little sister.

"I thought you said marshmallows didn't belong in pancakes," Michelle said.

"That's right. *In* the pancakes is bad, because it gets the pan all gooey. But *on*—after the pancakes are out of the pan and on a plate—is okay."

Hold it, Stephanie told herself. *Don't slip into the bossy zone. You promised.*

"Uhhh—what I mean is—go for it, Michelle." She tossed the bag of marshmallows to her sister. "Go marshmallow crazy."

Michelle smiled, a smile so wide, it almost touched her ears.

"Gosh. If I knew marshmallows would make you this happy, I would have let you have them months ago," Stephanie joked.

"I'm not happy because of the marshmallows. Although, I like them—and thanks and everything," Michelle said. "Actually, I'm happy because I came up with an amazing idea for a way to help Samantha!"

"You did?" Stephanie asked with surprise. "What is it?"

"I'm going to put on a show. I'm going to do everything—come up with the acts, direct the whole thing, probably even star in it," Michelle answered. "Cassie and Mandy and a bunch of my other friends are going to help. We're going to sell tickets and earn a ton of money for Samantha's operation."

"That's really—ummmmm—sweet of you," Stephanie said slowly. She poured more batter onto the skillet.

Stephanie did think it was sweet of Michelle. She also thought it was a pretty silly idea. Michelle had no clue how to put on a show that people would actually pay money to see.

She started to tell Michelle that maybe she should just send Samantha a nice card or something. Save herself the work. Then she remembered her promise to be less bossy.

She decided to keep her mouth shut.

"So do you want to be in it?" Michelle

asked. "I'll come up with a really great part for you—since you're my sister."

"That's really sweet of you," Stephanie said again. It was all she could think of *to* say, since she'd decided not to act like the know-it-all big sister.

"Then, you'll do it?" Michelle exclaimed. "You'll be in my show with me?"

Ugh. *There is no way, no possible way, I'm going to run around onstage with a bunch of nine-year-olds,* Stephanie thought. *Talk about major humiliation!*

"We'll have to start working on your act right away," Michelle rushed on. "I want to put on the show two weeks from now."

Two weeks? Stephanie thought. *That's insane.* Two weeks wasn't nearly long enough to pull together the kind of show Michelle was discussing.

She took a deep breath and reminded herself that this was *Michelle's* project.

"Um, I'm really crazed with school stuff right now," Stephanie said. "I don't think I'll have time to be in the show."

She slid another pancake onto Michelle's plate. Michelle stared down at it in silence.

Is she upset? Stephanie wondered. *But, I thought she wanted me to let her do things on her own.*

"Put me down for a ticket, though, okay?" Stephanie said. She shot another glance at Michelle. Her little sister continued to stare at the pancake.

"A ticket for every performance, I mean," Stephanie added. "I'm sure your show will be so good, I'll want to see it again and again."

Michelle looked up at her and smiled. "Thanks, Steph! Samantha and I *both* thank you for your support! You won't be disappointed, I promise."

Stephanie gave a chuckle. Michelle was so excited her words were tumbling out one after the other. "I'll make sure you get a seat right up front every time! Really! Since I'm in charge, that will be no problem." Michelle finally took a breath.

Stephanie reached out and gave Michelle's ponytail a playful tug. "Thanks," she said. "I guess I'm lucky to be related to the director."

"And star, and choreographer, and poster designer," Michelle said.

Stephanie thought about telling her that all those jobs were a lot for one person to handle.

But she didn't.

Because that would be bossy, and that was not how Stephanie wanted to be with Michelle.

"Want some of my yogurt?" Stephanie's best friend, Allie Taylor, asked her. She held out a large cup and spoon.

"Ugh!" Stephanie groaned. "No thanks!"

"I'll have some!" Darcy Powell declared. She shoveled a big scoop of chocolate chip yogurt into her mouth.

Normally, sharing a frozen yogurt with her friends in the mall was totally cool. But the pancake sundae Stephanie had had that morning, complete with frozen yogurt, chocolate chips, raisins, and granola, felt as if it had hardened inside her stomach.

The three girls stood in line on the lower level of the atrium, waiting to see Peace Smith. At the head of the line, near the big fountain, was the table where Peace was signing autographs.

Stephanie knew the pancakes weren't entirely to blame for her stomachache. She was also nervous about seeing Peace.

"I have no idea what I'm going to say to Heather—I mean Peace," Stephanie told her best friends.

"Well, we have a little more time to figure it out," Allie said. She peered up the long row of kids ahead of them.

"I don't know why you're worried," Darcy told them. "You both *know* her. What am I supposed to say? Hi, you might remember me from . . . nowhere? And by the way, someday I aspire to be . . . well, you."

Stephanie and Allie hadn't met Darcy until she started at their school in the fourth grade. That was years after Heather and her family moved to Los Angeles. So Darcy had never met her before.

The line moved up a couple of feet and Stephanie's whole stomach—not just the pancake sundae—started to feel as if it had turned to stone.

"She's so gorgeous," Allie said. She stood on tiptoe to get a better look. "I mean, that long, thick brown hair, and those eyes.

They're so green, they practically look fake. No wonder she's almost a star."

"I don't think she's almost a star anymore," Darcy said. "She was almost a star when she did that hair gel commercial. Now she's been on *Summer's Cove*."

"Yeah. She's definitely a full-out star now," Stephanie agreed. *Summer's Cove* was the most popular teen soap ever. If you were on the show, you were *it* with a capital *I*.

So, why would "it-girl" Peace Smith want to talk to me—Stephanie Tanner, the definitely "not-even-close-to-it-girl"? Stephanie thought.

The line moved forward again. Now even Stephanie's feet felt like stone. She could hardly move them.

Darcy grabbed her arm and gave her a tug. "Come on. We're next!" she whispered.

Stephanie found herself face-to-face with Peace Smith. What should she say? What should she say?

"Hi! Remember us?" Allie burst out.

A tiny wrinkle appeared between Peace's eyebrows. She obviously had no idea who they were. Stephanie had to jump in to save the situation.

33

"Uh, first grade," she began. "We helped you get back at Nathan Frieder when he stuck your braid in paste."

Eeeew! Not exactly the clever, sophisticated remark she wanted to make.

Stephanie grimaced. Her cheeks felt as if they were on fire.

"Allie? Stephanie?" Peace asked. "Wow! Of course I remember you!"

She squealed. Then she jumped up from her seat, leaned across the table, and grabbed them in a double hug. "It's so fantastic to see you!"

Stephanie's whole body suddenly relaxed. *Cool!* Peace remembered her!

"This is our friend Darcy," she told Peace. "She's a big fan."

"It's great to meet you," Peace said.

Darcy stared at Peace, her mouth hanging open.

Stephanie giggled. Darcy was usually so outspoken. It was weird to see her speechless.

"So are you just in town for the day?" Allie asked.

Peace shook her head. "Actually, I'm spending the semester here. I'm going to acting school part of the day, then I'm getting tutored so I won't get behind in my regular school-work."

"Sounds intense," Stephanie said. She could hardly believe she was chatting away with Peace Smith. It was so cool!

"What kind of acting classes are you—" Allie began.

Before she could finish her question, a man in a suit stepped up to Peace and whispered something in her ear.

Peace gave Stephanie, Darcy, and Allie an apologetic smile. "I'm sorry, guys. I can't really talk right now. There are a lot of people waiting. I want to make sure I get to them all."

"Of course," Stephanie said. "We understand." She plastered a big smile on her face. "Well, bye!"

"Bye," Allie and Darcy echoed.

"Thanks so much for coming," Peace said.

Stephanie started off through the crowd. "Imagine," she said to her friends, "Peace Smith right here in our neighborhood."

"Yeah," Darcy finally spoke up. "San Francisco kids will probably never get a chance to see her this up-close-and-personal again."

Stephanie stopped in her tracks. An idea hit her.

"Unless . . ." she said. She spun around and rushed back to Peace's table.

"Did you forget something?" Darcy called as she and Allie scrambled after Stephanie.

"Not exactly," Stephanie said. She waited until Peace signed some drooling guy's T-shirt, then she hurried back up to the table.

Some of the people in line yelled out protests, but Stephanie ignored them. This was too important!

"Sorry to bother you again, Peace, but there's something I wanted to ask you," Stephanie said in a rush. "A kind of favor."

She knew if she gave herself time to think about what she was about to do, she'd chicken out, so she pushed ahead.

"My sister and I are putting on a show to earn money so that a sick little girl can get an operation. I was wondering if you'd be in it?" she blurted out.

Peace stared at her a moment, clearly startled.

For a split second Stephanie imagined herself hanging out on a regular basis with Peace—an actual star. It would be so cool! Plus it would help Michelle make tons of money for Samantha's cause.

Please say yes, Stephanie silently begged. *Please!*

Chapter 5

I can't believe it!" Stephanie muttered, half in shock. She sat with her friends in a booth in the mall's food court. "I can't believe Peace agreed to be in the show!"

"I just have one question—what show?" Darcy demanded. She took a sip of her diet soda.

"Yeah, and what sick little girl?" Allie chimed in. "You've been holding out on us. Spill, Stephanie."

Stephanie sat back in her seat, taking in the moment.

It was amazing. She pictured all her friends from school finding out that *she* was friends with Peace Smith. And not only that, she had gotten the star to perform in *her* show!

People would be begging to help out with the talent show now. As a bonus, Stephanie's popularity would rocket through the roof!

"I'm serious, Stephanie," Allie warned. "Start talking."

"Peace Smith is going to be in our show!" Stephanie repeated.

"What show are you talking about?" Darcy exploded.

Stephanie took a deep breath and explained. She started with the video of Samantha O'Reilly and ended with the conversation she had had with Michelle that morning.

"So it's really Michelle's show," Allie said when she finished. "That's not what you told Peace."

Stephanie felt a stab of guilt as she remembered Michelle's words—about how she planned to be the director, the choreographer, the poster designer, and the star of the show.

That would all have to change now that Peace was involved.

"Well, it was Michelle's *idea*," Stephanie admitted. "But she asked me to help her out.

And there was no way I could tell Peace the show was my little sister's idea. A star like Peace would never agree to perform with a bunch of kids."

"I guess that's true," Allie said. "And having Peace star in the show will definitely sell a ton of tickets. Much more than if it was just Michelle and her friends."

"And that's the point, right?" Darcy added. "To earn money for Samantha's operation."

"Exactly," Stephanie answered. She smiled, already feeling less guilty.

It was cool that she and Peace would have the chance to hang out together, but helping Michelle to raise money for Samantha was the coolest.

"You know, even though Michelle wants to do everything herself, there's no way she can handle putting on a professional-style production," Stephanie continued. "Not even with all her friends helping."

"Even for us it will be a challenge," Allie agreed. She reached into her mini-backpack and pulled out a notepad. "In fact, we should probably get started right now. Let's make a list of things to do to get this show off the ground."

"First, we should probably call all the kids we know with talent and recruit them," Stephanie said. "Michelle and her friends can do some acts. They'd be cute. But we need some real talent, too. Besides Peace, I mean."

"Wait. Before we start all that, let's talk about the whole talent show idea," Darcy said.

Stephanie could tell from the way Darcy spoke that she didn't think a talent show was the best idea.

"It does seem kind of elementary-school," Allie admitted.

"Plus a talent show wouldn't give Peace a big enough part," Stephanie agreed. "I think we should come up with something that will keep her onstage most of the time."

"She's the one people will be coming to see. Everyone else will be like part of the set or something," Allie agreed.

"Maybe we could do a play that's sort of like *Summer's Cove*," Darcy suggested. "You could write it, Steph. Just put in lots of jealous boyfriends and crazy parents."

Stephanie cracked up. "I would love to write something like that," she answered.

"But we don't have time. We need to start rehearsing right away. Coming up with an original play would take too long."

"On that TV show *Show-Biz Today*, I saw clips from the Broadway revival of *Grease*," Darcy said. "Maybe we could do a shortened version of that. Lots of singing and dancing, with some quick lines of dialogue in between."

"Yeah! I could definitely write little scenes to move the story from song to song," Stephanie said. "And the part of Sandy would be perfect for Peace!"

"I bet we could get the school band to play for us," Allie jumped in. "And a lot of the people in choir would want to be in the chorus, I bet."

"The drill team probably has a lot of good dancers who would be into performing," Stephanie said. She was getting totally excited by the idea.

Grease, starring Peace Smith and directed by Stephanie Tanner, was going to be excellent!

"We'd probably even be able to convince a lot of guys to perform," Darcy added. "The male characters in *Grease* are pretty cool. And the costumes are just jeans and T-shirts and leather jackets. Nothing for the guys to whine about."

"Are you kidding? Once they hear Peace Smith is in it, they'll be dying to sign up!" Stephanie said. "They'd probably wear tights if they had to."

"You're right!" Allie exclaimed. "Our rehearsals are going to be the most popular spot in town. Everyone's going to want the chance to hang out with Peace."

And I'll get to spend more time with her than anyone, Stephanie thought. *Because I'm organizing the whole thing*.

"So we have our Sandy. But who is going to be Danny?" Darcy asked.

"It has to be somebody cool," Stephanie answered.

"And somebody with good breath—since the guy is going to have to kiss Peace," Allie joked.

"How about Eli Sanderson?" Darcy suggested. "I saw him in his school's production of *Guys and Dolls*. He was awesome."

Stephanie and Allie stared at her.

"What?" Stephanie asked.

4 3

"What?" Allie said at the same time. "Eli Sanderson is a senior in high school. He's totally cute, and he's the most popular guy ever. He's not going to be in a show put on by us!"

"Even if he gets to kiss Peace?" Darcy reminded them.

Stephanie smiled. "Darcy's right. Of course he'll do it."

"Peace Smith and Eli Sanderson," Allie said. "Whew!"

"Let's go ask Eli right now," Darcy exclaimed. "He works at the sporting goods store."

"And after that we should go to the vintage clothing store," Allie said. "I think they have some of those fifties-style skirts. You know, the poofy ones that have poodles on the front. Maybe they'd even lend them to us if we explain that the show is for Samantha."

Uh-oh, Stephanie thought. *Before Darcy and Allie plan the entire show, I'd better talk to Michelle. Pronto.*

Chapter
6

Michelle stared at the drawing she'd just finished and smiled. Her costume design still needed a little work, but it was getting better.

She could already picture herself in the lavender leotard with the short purple skirt. The beads she planned on sewing around the neck and wrists would glitter in the spotlight. And everyone in the audience would be staring at her as she led the big tap number she planned.

Michelle closed her eyes and imagined the number. She struck her final pose—and the audience applauded wildly. Then they gave her a standing ovation!

"Thank you," Michelle whispered, trying to sound modest. She smooched her palm, then blew the kiss to her adoring fans. "You are such a wonderful audience. I love you all."

"I love you, too." A voice interrupted Michelle's daydream.

Michelle opened her eyes. Stephanie stood in the doorway, her arms folded.

Michelle smiled, feeling sort of silly. "How long have you been standing there?" she asked.

"Long enough," Stephanie said. Grinning, she sat down on her bed. "So, what have you been up to all day?"

Michelle blinked. Stephanie hardly ever had time to hang out in their room and talk. She was always busy—getting ready to go out with her friends, working on an article for her school paper, or trying to figure out what to say to some guy on the phone.

"I've been designing costumes for the show," Michelle answered.

"Can I see?" Stephanie asked.

"Sure!" Michelle was dying to show off her sketches. She grabbed her drawing pad off her desk and sat down next to Stephanie. "This one is for the big tap number. It's going to be right before intermission."

"Uh-huh. Nice," Stephanie said.

Michelle glanced at her sister. For some reason, she had the feeling Stephanie wasn't looking at the drawing. "Stephanie, what's up with you?" she asked.

"I got to talk to Peace Smith at the mall today," Stephanie blurted out.

"Cool! So, was I right? Did she remember you?" Michelle asked.

Stephanie nodded. "She not only remembered me, she agreed to do me—and you—a gigantic favor!" Stephanie gave a little bounce on the bed.

"What kind of favor?" Michelle asked.

"She wants to star in our show!" Stephanie exclaimed.

Michelle's mouth dropped open. Could it be true? A real live famous actress was going to be in her show?

"No way!" Michelle exclaimed.

"Yes way," Stephanie answered. "I told her all about Samantha O'Reilly, and she was totally into helping her."

"Awesome!" A real live famous actress was going to be in her show! Michelle felt more sure than ever that the whole project was going to be a huge success. With someone like Peace Smith involved, there was no limit to the amount of money they could make for Samantha's operation!

Michelle glanced down again at her costume design. She liked it. But maybe to a professional actress it wouldn't seem quite special enough.

"Do you think Peace would like this outfit? It's what everyone in the number is going to wear," she asked Stephanie. "Maybe for a big star like Peace, it needs more beads. Or sequins."

Michelle grabbed one of her glitter markers and added a row of sparkly sequins to the hem of the skirt. She frowned. It still didn't seem quite right—quite special enough.

"I think it's fine, but—" Stephanie began.

"I know! I'll pick flowers and make a giant wreath out of them for our heads!" Michelle exclaimed.

"What number did you say this costume is for?" Stephanie asked.

Michelle sighed. Wasn't Stephanie listening? "I already told you," she answered. "It's for the big tap number."

"Oh, right," Stephanie said. "So—is that the only number you have planned so far?"

"Are you kidding?" Michelle asked. "Mandy and Cassie came over while you were out at the mall. We got almost the whole show planned out."

Michelle consulted her list. "We're going to start off with a tap dance. I'm going to dance to "Singin' in the Rain" while Mandy and Cassie twirl umbrellas on either side of me."

Stephanie nodded. "That's a cute idea, Michelle. But now that Peace is going to be in the show, you have to think about where she'll fit in."

Michelle shrugged. "Well, Peace could twirl an umbrella, too. Or maybe she could hold an umbrella over my head while I dance—you know, to make the rain part seem more real and—"

"Don't you think people might be disappointed if they buy a ticket to see Peace and then all she does is hold an umbrella?" Stephanie interrupted.

"She'd get her own act, too, of course," Michelle answered. "Do you have her phone number? I'll call her and ask what she's good at. Then we'll come up with some ideas for her. Oh! Did I tell you we have a lion tamer act? It's going to be hilarious. Lee's going to put ruffles on the collar of his aunt's Chihuahua and—"

"One number for Peace isn't going to be enough," Stephanie said, cutting her off.

"So she can do two," Michelle shot back. "She can do a—"

"I'm sorry, but I don't think you're getting it," Stephanie broke in.

Michelle shot her sister an annoyed glance. That was the third time Stephanie had interrupted her, and Michelle did *not* like being interrupted.

"You didn't even let me finish," she snapped.

"I didn't have to," Stephanie answered. "It doesn't matter what the two numbers are. *Two* numbers aren't enough for the star of the show."

The star? Michelle thought. When did Peace go from being in the show to being *the star?*

50

"It's a talent show," Michelle reminded Stephanie. "One person can't be in every—"

"Exactly," Stephanie interrupted *again*. "So maybe we shouldn't do a talent show. I have another idea. We'll do a bunch of numbers from *Grease*, with little scenes in between them to move the cast from one song to the next."

"*You* have an idea?" Michelle repeated. "Why are *you* having ideas about *my* show?"

"I realized that you could use some help," Stephanie answered. "I know I said that I was busy with school, but I decided that I'd make time to work on the show. After all, it's for such a worthy cause."

"And now I'm supposed to throw away everything Cassie and Mandy and I planned so that we can do what *you* want?" Michelle demanded.

This was too much, Michelle thought. *Too, too much. Just yesterday, Stephanie had promised to be less bossy. Now she was trying to take over everything!*

"Think about it," Stephanie argued. "Your

talent show needs a ton of different sets and costumes to look good. With the *Grease* idea, most of the costumes could be the same for every number. The sets, too. Since we want to do the show as soon as possible, that's stuff we have to think about."

Michelle sat silent for a moment. What Stephanie said made sense. She had to admit it.

"Besides, everyone would buy a ticket for *Grease* starring Peace Smith. Everyone!" Stephanie added. "And that means more money for Samantha."

Samantha. Michelle reminded herself. *That's what this is all about. Samantha.*

Stephanie was only trying to help. Just like Michelle.

"You really think *Grease* will sell more tickets than a talent show?"

"Absolutely!" Stephanie answered.

"Okay, then we're doing *Grease!*" Michelle exclaimed.

Stephanie jumped up from the bed. "All right! Grease *is the word, is the word, is the word,*" she sang as she danced her way out the door.

Let's Put On a Show

Michelle sighed and flipped to a fresh page on her drawing pad. She had a whole new set of costumes to design.

Maybe Peace would like a leather jacket—with sequins! she thought. She smiled as she started to draw.

Chapter 7

Sit right here, Michelle," Cassie called out. She practically had to yell to be heard over the crowd of kids swarming around Michelle's backyard.

Michelle smiled when she saw the sign Cassie had taped to the back of the chair. It said DIRECTOR.

"Okay, people, listen up," she called as she settled into the chair. "You already know that Peace Smith is going to be in our show. Once she auditions, she'll probably get the part of Sandy. Today we're going to have auditions for the part of Danny. He's the cool guy who falls in love with Sandy. Up first is—"

Mandy handed Michelle a clipboard with a list of names on it. "Up first is Jamar Anderson," Michelle continued. "Everyone settle down so we can hear Jamar sing."

"Wait. I have to *sing?*" Jamar yelped as he stepped into the clear space in front of Michelle's chair. He nervously played with the zipper of his leather jacket.

"Of course you have to sing," Cassie answered. "We're doing *Grease!*"

"All he's thinking about is *Peace,*" Lee Wagner shouted out. He was dressed in jeans and a white T-shirt with rolled-up sleeves.

"Lee, what do you have in your hair?" Michelle asked. She gazed at Lee's black hair, which now looked kind of gray.

"My mom told me that guys in the fifties used to slick their hair down with grease. That's why the play is called that," Lee explained. "We didn't have any hair grease in the house, so I just used butter! Cool, huh?"

Eeew! Michelle thought. She shuddered. She had to give Lee an A for effort, but she'd have to remind him not to use any butter the day of the actual show.

Michelle returned her attention to Jamar. He

looked embarrassed. He zipped his leather jacket all the way up, then unzipped it a second later.

"Jamar, I'm sorry you didn't know about the singing, but if you want a chance at the part of Danny, you're going to have to try," Michelle told him. "Sing anything. It doesn't have to be from the show."

Jamar zipped his jacket back up. He opened his mouth. Closed it. Opened it again.

Then he started singing the ABCs—in a high, squeaky voice.

Michelle bit on the inside of her cheek to keep from giggling. She made a note next to his name—nonsinging part only. She let him get to Z, then interrupted.

"Okay, that's fine, thank you," she exclaimed. "We'll let you know."

I'm really getting the hang of this director stuff, Michelle thought. *Maybe someday I'll be the director of a show on Broadway.*

"It was the only song I could think of," Jamar mumbled. He yanked on his zipper again, and it jammed.

"It was fine," Mandy told him.

Michelle gave him a pat on the shoulder as he walked by. "Good try, Jamar."

"Hey! Why don't you help me build the sets?" Cassie added.

"I want to help build sets, too," Erin Davis called.

"Don't worry, I need all the help I can get," Cassie answered.

"What about posters?" Karlee Johnson called. "I've got this great art software on my computer. I could come up with something awesome."

Everyone started talking at once. Someone was volunteering to do an e-mail flyer for the show. Someone was saying she wanted to help sew the poodle skirts. And someone was saying the show should be put on in the community center basketball court, with the audience sitting in the bleachers.

Michelle stood up. She cupped her hands around her mouth. "Quiet!" she bellowed.

The backyard instantly went silent.

Cool! Michelle smiled to herself. She had a feeling she was going to like being a director—very much.

"We have only two weeks—a little less than two weeks, actually, to get this show on its feet," Michelle said.

She glanced from face to face, making eye contact with as many kids as she could. "First we're going to finish our auditions. Then Cassie, Mandy, and I will take names of people who want to work on costumes, posters, ticket sales, and set construction."

"I'll do ticket sales instead of posters," Karlee piped up. "I love to talk on the phone!"

"That's great, Karlee," Michelle called. "But like I just said, we'll deal with all that after the auditions."

"Shouldn't we at least figure out where we're having the show?" Jeff Farrington asked. "We can't do posters or anything until we know that."

"Hey, who's the director here?" Michelle asked.

"Ummm—wait a minute. Don't tell me." Jeff scratched his head.

Michelle giggled. Jeff was so funny. No wonder he had a reputation as the class clown.

He snapped his fingers. "I've got it. You're the director, Michelle!"

"That's right," she answered. Then she

grinned at him. "And your director has already found a place for the show. I talked to Ms. Daily, the music teacher, and she said we can use our school auditorium."

"All right!" Jamar yelled. "Way to go, Michelle."

"You rock, Michelle!" Jeff added.

I guess I showed them that I know exactly what I'm doing! Michelle thought.

She checked her clipboard. "We have seven more potential Dannys to audition. Let's get started."

"I thought I already had the part," an older voice called out. "No one said anything to me about auditioning."

Michelle turned in her seat. She saw Stephanie standing in the kitchen doorway with a huge, totally handsome guy.

"You do have the part," Stephanie answered.

Huh? Michelle thought.

"Everybody, come on outside!" Stephanie called into the house. She held the door open, and tons of teenagers started trooping into the backyard, joining Michelle's group.

Michelle recognized some of them—like

Stephanie's best friends, Allie and Darcy. But most of them she'd never seen before.

Michelle jumped up and pushed her way over to Stephanie. "What's going on?" she demanded. "Why are all these people here? And who is that guy who said he had the part of Danny?"

"Now that Peace is the star of the show, I figured you would need some extra help," Stephanie told Michelle. "So I brought some."

"We do have a lot of stuff to tackle before the show," Michelle muttered. She tried to ignore the way her stomach was twisting itself into a pretzel. "But, Steph, what did that guy mean?"

Stephanie shot a look at the dark-haired boy. "That's Eli Sanderson," she said, keeping her voice low. "He's the most popular guy at the high school. With him as Danny, the show will be sold out every performance."

"But you already said it would be sold out, anyway, because of Peace," Michelle pointed out. "I don't think it's fair for him to get the part without even auditioning."

Stephanie took another glance at Eli. "Get real, Michelle," she said. "Don't you think it would be kind of silly for Peace and a ten-year-old boy to play girlfriend and boyfriend?"

Michelle glanced down at her shoes. "I didn't really think about that," she admitted.

Stephanie slung an arm around her shoulder. "That's what big sisters are for," she said. "To think of things like that. Now, take a look at Eli. Didn't I find you the most gorgeous Danny ever?"

Michelle peeked at Eli from under her eyelashes. She had to admit—he *was* pretty cute. "Can he sing?" she asked.

"Of course. He'll be perfect. I promise," Stephanie said. "I have more great news for you, too. But let me tell everyone at the same time."

Stephanie strode across the lawn—and sat down in Michelle's chair.

Her *director's* chair.

"Stephanie, wait! That's my—" Michelle called. It was too late. Her sister had already taken Michelle's special seat.

She strode over to a spot next to Stephanie. Cassie and Mandy fell in beside her.

"What's going on?" Cassie asked.

61

"Can I have everyone's attention, please?" Stephanie called before Michelle could answer. "We've got a lot of ground to cover."

Michelle positioned herself right next to Stephanie. *I'm still the director,* she told herself. *Steph's just helping out a little.*

"I'm happy to report that Mr. Lang has agreed to let us use the new high school auditorium for the show," Stephanie announced.

All the older kids, Stephanie's friends, let out a big cheer.

"But wait a minute! Michelle already got permission to use the auditorium at our school," Jeff called out.

"The lighting and sound equipment at the high school is brand-new, and the auditorium can seat over five hundred people," Stephanie answered. "I think that's more like the kind of theater our show deserves, don't you?"

A chorus of *yeahs* erupted—mainly from the older kids.

"It will be totally cool!" Darcy exclaimed. "Like performing on Broadway!"

"Is the auditorium switch okay with you, Michelle?" Mandy whispered.

Michelle pictured the auditorium at her

school. It was small. And there was only one spotlight. She had to admit that the place was hardly high-tech.

"Stephanie's auditorium sounds great," Michelle answered.

It would have been nice of Stephanie to check with me before she made other plans, Michelle thought. *After all, this is my show.*

But what did it matter, really? Michelle still had a zillion things to handle—like designing the costumes, working out the dance numbers, overseeing the posters, the sets, and the ticket sales.

"There's more, guys," Stephanie rushed on. "The vintage clothing store in the mall is going to lend us all the fifties stuff we need for costumes. Darcy's going to coordinate times for everyone to go in and try on outfits."

"Wow! That store is the coolest," Michelle's friend Erin shouted.

Michelle frowned. *Erin must have forgotten that she said my designs were the coolest when I showed them to her at school today.*

Suddenly Michelle didn't feel like a director anymore. Instead, she felt like Stephanie Tanner's little sister. Period.

Cassie nudged Michelle. "Aren't you going to tell Stephanie that you already came up with costume designs?" she asked.

"The vintage store has real clothes from the fifties," Michelle muttered. "They'll be better than the ones we could make."

"On to advertising," Stephanie said. "I talked to a reporter at the *San Francisco Chronicle*—a friend of my journalism teacher's. She's going to run a story about how we're doing the show to earn money for Samantha's operation. And my dad and my aunt Becky are going to mention our show on their show. Plus we have the most fabulous posters! Hold one up, Allie!"

Allie reached into the big cardboard box at her feet and pulled out a hot-pink poster that had a couple dancing on the hood of a car on the front. Peace Smith's name was printed in huge letters.

"I want each of you to take ten posters and put them up ASAP," Stephanie told the group. "I divided the town into sections so that we won't be covering the same area twice."

Michelle sat down on the grass next to

Stephanie's chair. She was feeling kind of dizzy. How did Stephanie make all this happen so fast?

"Why did you get posters made?" Michelle asked her sister. "Mandy was already handling that."

"Don't you like them?" Stephanie asked. "I got one of the best art students in school to do the design. He worked all day on Sunday and we got them printed up today."

"Luckily one of my friends' mom runs a copy shop," Allie explained. "So these didn't cost us anything. She did tickets for us, too."

"I guess they're nice, but—" Michelle began.

"Okay, then," Stephanie interrupted. She turned back to the crowd in front of her. "Whenever you put up a poster, I want you to take ten tickets with you. I expect everyone to sell their ten tickets, then come back for another poster, and another ten tickets. Whoever sells the most tickets by show time will win an autographed picture of Peace."

"Yeah!" the crowd cheered.

Michelle's friend Jeff dropped down on the

grass next to Michelle. "Your sister is amazing," he said. "She thought of absolutely everything."

Yeah, everything, Michelle thought, *except the fact that she's just totally taken over my show!*

STEPHANIE

Chapter
8

Stephanie ducked into the bathroom of the high school auditorium. She'd been running around like crazy, trying to get everything set up for their first rehearsal.

Now she just wanted to grab a second to put on a fresh coat of lip gloss and brush her hair. Peace always looked so amazing that Stephanie didn't want to look like a total mess when Peace showed up.

She stepped in front of one of the mirrors and pulled out her brush. Before she could run it through her hair even once, Michelle burst in.

"Where's Peace?" she demanded. "We can't start without her. After all, *she's* the star."

Stephanie frowned at Michelle's snotty tone of voice. Her little sister had a major attitude ever since they got to rehearsal.

Michelle thought the sheet music was too blurry to read. Then she thought the seats in the auditorium were too hard. *Then* she thought the piano sounded funny.

"Well, where is she?" Michelle repeated. "You must know. *You're* the one who wants to be in charge of everything!"

"I don't want to be in charge of everything," Stephanie said for what felt like the millionth time. "I just don't think you're ready to run a whole show by yourself. Why is it so hard for you to admit that you need my help?"

"Because I don't," Michelle muttered.

"Oh, right. It would have been great to see a ten-year-old with butter in his hair doing a romantic scene with Peace Smith," Stephanie shot back.

"At least Lee showed up on time," Michelle snapped.

Stephanie checked her watch. "Peace is only a few minutes late. Why don't you hand out the lyric sheets to everyone. They can get started learning the words to the songs until she gets here."

"Uh, I'm here already," a voice said from the last stall.

"Oh, well—uh—take your time," Stephanie answered.

How totally and completely humiliating! Stephanie wanted to sink into the floor. Peace had heard her and her little sister talking about her! She hoped Peace would understand that Michelle was little—and just being difficult.

"Michelle, go into the auditorium and tell my friend Colin that I want the spotlight on Peace when she walks in," Stephanie said. She struggled to keep her voice calm.

Michelle rolled her eyes, but she left without a word.

For once! Stephanie thought.

The door to Peace's bathroom stall swung open, and she stepped out. "You don't have to make a big production out of my being here or anything," she told Stephanie. "I mean, it's not like I'm actually *famous*. I've just been in a couple of shows and commercials."

"You're famous to everyone here, and

you're the star of the show," Stephanie declared. "Everyone should know it!"

Peace shrugged. "Whatever you say, Steph. You're the boss."

Stephanie felt a goofy grin of pleasure spread across her face. Who would have ever thought a celebrity like Peace Smith would say something like that to Stephanie Tanner?

"I, um, saw the posters on my way in," Peace said.

"Don't they look awesome?" Stephanie exclaimed.

"Really professional," Peace agreed. "It's just that . . . I was thinking the show was a regular play. You know, not a musical."

"I know the part of Sandy is probably not as dramatic as the roles you play in your drama classes," Stephanie said quickly. "But it will be fun. I guarantee it. You'll get to sing all those great songs. And you'll get to dance with Eli Sanderson."

"The guy you showed me in the yearbook?" Peace asked. Stephanie nodded.

"He is pretty adorable," Peace admitted.

"I get the feeling that he thinks so, too,"

Stephanie filled Peace in. "But I guess nobody's perfect."

"You should have seen the guy in the Zap commercial. He was mega-conceited," Peace said. "Like he thought being in a hair gel commercial would make him the next Tom Cruise or something."

Stephanie laughed. *Wow!* she thought. *I'm actually standing in the bathroom talking about boys with Peace Smith!*

By the end of the show, we could be really great friends. We could keep in touch. Maybe she'd invite me to parties in L.A. and—

"I guess we should go in, huh?" Peace asked, pulling Stephanie away from her daydreams.

Stephanie hurried over to the door and jerked it open. "After you, O famous one," she joked.

Joked! With Peace Smith!

"Oh, no, no, no, no, no. After *you*," Peace replied.

Stephanie blinked at her. "You remember that?" she cried. It was something she, Peace, and Allie used to do in the first grade. Every time the three of them came to a door together, each girl would insist that the other go first, until everyone couldn't help laughing.

"Of course I remember it," Peace said. "Except I don't remember exactly why we started doing it."

"Me neither," Stephanie admitted. She led the way to the auditorium door. "You have to go first this time," she said seriously, "for the spotlight. Go right up on the stage, okay?"

"Okay." Peace took a deep breath. Then she pushed open the double doors and stepped through. She had a big smile on her face when the spotlight hit her. Stephanie thought she looked absolutely dazzling.

"Everybody, meet our star," Stephanie called as she followed Peace inside and up to the stage.

"Peace, Peace, Peace," one of the boys started chanting.

Seconds later everyone joined in. "Peace, Peace, Peace!"

Peace made a little quiet-down gesture with her hands. "Hi, guys," she called out. "It's nice to meet you all. I'm really excited about the show."

"And I hope you're all excited about our

first rehearsal!" Stephanie jumped in. "We're going to start with a sing-through. Just stand up and we'll sing all the songs one by one, including the solos."

"Ummm—Stephanie, that's moving things along a little too quickly for me," Peace said. "I can't really sing the songs until I know who my character is. My new acting teacher says I should keep a diary—and write it as whatever character I play. I haven't had the chance to do that for Sandy yet, and I need to before I do anything else."

"But the first performance is in a week and a half," Michelle called out from the first row. "We have to start rehearsing *now* or we're never going to be ready in time."

Clearly, Stephanie realized, this kind of exercise was really important to a serious actress like Peace. Michelle might not understand it, but after all, Stephanie was the older sister, older and wiser.

"Okay," Stephanie said. "Peace will go back into her dressing room and work on her diary. And the rest of us will do the sing-through without her. We'll all just sing Sandy's part together."

"Thanks, Steph," Peace said. "You're the greatest!" She hurried offstage.

Michelle charged up the steps and marched over to Stephanie. "I can't believe you aren't making her sing with us," she said quietly.

"Michelle, you have no idea what a real artist like Peace needs to do to get ready to perform," Stephanie told her. "You have to give your actors some space. You have to trust them if you want to be a great director."

"You mean like you?" Michelle asked sarcastically.

"Would you just give me a break?" Stephanie asked. "I promise you I'm going to make this show the best anyone has ever seen. And Peace will be amazing in it."

Michelle gave a disgusted snort. "Not if she doesn't practice."

"Michelle, I know exactly what I'm doing," Stephanie said firmly. "Trust me."

Chapter
9

Two days later Michelle sat down in her usual seat in the front row of the auditorium. The guys were rehearsing their "Greased Lightning" number, and it would probably be a while before they finished.

I may as well get some homework done, Michelle thought. *I'm not rehearsing right now. And it's not like Stephanie will actually let me do anything else.*

She pulled her binder out of her backpack and flipped it open. A piece of paper fluttered down to the floor. Michelle picked it up. It was one of her director's to-do lists.

"Arrrggh!" she grumbled. She crumpled it

up and jammed it deep into her pack. She wouldn't be needing it. This show was nothing like the one she'd planned. And even though Stephanie called her the co-director, Michelle wasn't fooled.

She was co-big-fat-nothing. She could leave right then and no one would miss her. Well, there would be a little hole in the dance numbers she was in, but that would be easy for Stephanie, director of the whole entire planet, to fix.

Yeah, maybe she *should* leave right now.

Except . . .

Except that there *was* one person who was counting on her to be there. One very important person.

Michelle reached into her backpack again and pulled out a bright blue envelope. She slid out the sheet of bright blue stationery inside.

She had already read the letter about six times, but she needed to read it again. Reading it was the only thing that was going to get her through the second week of rehearsals and the three performances of the show.

Let's Put On a Show

Dear Michelle,

I still can't believe that you and your friends are putting on a show to help me! You are really the best! I can't wait to get the video of the show that you promised!

I know you told me in your last letter that Peace Smith is going to perform in the show. That's really cool. It will be fun to watch her, but I'm going to spend most of my time watching you.

It's kind of silly, but I feel like you and I are almost like sisters or something. I mean, we both have the same favorite colors, we both have golden retrievers (your dad told me that), and we both love to dance.

So when I watch you on the tape, it will be a little bit like watching me up there onstage. It will be a little like I'm actually dancing, which is one of the things I don't get to do anymore. Is that totally weird? Or do you know what I mean?

I have to go now. I have *another* doctor's appointment. Majorly boring.

My mom and dad say thanks so much

for helping to earn money for my surgery. And I say thanks, too. Even my dog, Ringo, says thanks. (But he says it in a barking kind of way that only I understand! Ha-ha!)

Lots of love,
Samantha

Michelle carefully refolded the letter, slid it back into the envelope, and returned it to her pack.

There's no way I can walk out on the show—no matter how mad I am at Steph, Michelle thought. *Samantha needs me. Especially because she wants to feel like she's up there onstage, too.*

"Hey, Michelle, have you seen Peace?" Allie whispered from the second row. "I finished shortening her skirt and I want her to try it on."

Michelle shook her head. "Sorry."

What is with Peace always being late? Michelle wondered. *Did she want to be in the show or not?*

One thing is for sure, she thought. *If I were the director—*

She cut herself off and sighed. Unfortunately, she wasn't the director. She was only the co-big-fat-nothing.

She reached into her backpack and grabbed her math workbook. She opened it, and realized she just wasn't in the mood for math.

"Guys, guys, guys, stop!" Stephanie shouted. Her voice was so loud, Michelle jumped and dropped her pen.

"Half of you are on the wrong foot. And half of you—I just don't know what you think you're doing, but it's not good," Stephanie continued. "Now, listen. It's right hand up. Left leg cross over. Left hand out. And then hip, hip."

The guys looked totally confused. Michelle shook her head. You couldn't *tell* people dance steps, you had to *show* them.

She felt like jumping up onstage and taking them through the routine herself. Stephanie would find something to complain about if she did. Every time Michelle had come up with a suggestion, Stephanie had found some reason why it wasn't right for *her* show.

"Michelle, stop whatever you're doing," Stephanie called. "Peace is here. We're going to work on the 'We Go Together' number."

"Fine," Michelle muttered. She slid the letter back into her binder. She stood up and headed for the steps leading to the stage. Peace walked up to the stage right in front of her.

Why is she wearing that wool scarf? Michelle wondered. It's not even a little cold in here.

"Hi, guys," Peace whispered when she reached the stage.

Whoa! Peace's voice sounded like a sick frog's.

"Hi, Peace!" Stephanie chirped. "Ready to practice the big finale?"

"Sorry, Stephanie. I can't talk. So I definitely can't sing," Peace whispered. "I have laryngitis."

"Oh, no!" Stephanie cried. "That's awful."

"I guess I can't rehearse today," Peace croaked.

First she has to do her stupid character diary, Michelle thought. *Now she's sick*. The show was in seven days, and Peace hadn't sung a note or danced a step. She hadn't even practiced with the rest of the group once! This was a disaster!

"Maybe we could just go through the dance part of the number," Stephanie suggested. "I mean, if you're feeling up to it."

"Sure. Of course. Just let me put on my dance shoes," Peace answered.

Peace rifled through her bag. "Uh, I don't seem to have . . ." She frowned as she rooted deeper into her backpack. Finally she looked up at Stephanie. "I can't believe this. I forgot my dance shoes!" she said.

"No problem," Stephanie said. "Not everyone has dance shoes. You can work in your regular ones."

Peace shook her head. She smiled an apologetic smile. "At my school they told us it's not good for our feet to dance without the right shoes."

Stephanie brushed her hair out of her face and slowly let out a breath. "Okay, well, why don't you watch the number so you can get really familiar with the steps," she suggested.

"Great!" Peace said. She hurried offstage and sat down in the front row.

"Okay, everybody!" Stephanie cried. "This is the last number of the show, and we want it to blow everyone away. We're not leaving here until we get it perfect!"

Too bad there's no way to get it perfect, Michelle thought, *without Peace.*

MICHELLE

Chapter
10

"That was better," Stephanie called after they'd done "We Go Together" for the fourth time. "But it still wasn't perfect. Again, everybody!"

She nodded at Mr. Lang, who was sitting at the piano at the edge of the stage. The high school music teacher nodded back and he started the song—*again*.

Michelle spun around to face Jeff, who was her partner for the number. They started to do the twist, keeping perfect time with the music.

"I want to see smiles," Stephanie cried. "Big smiles with tons of teeth!"

Jeff gave a strange grin that looked more like a scream of pain. Michelle could see every tooth in his head. Scary.

"Okay, first group, get ready to make your cross," Stephanie instructed. "And—go!"

Michelle led the way from stage right to stage left. She snapped her fingers with every step.

Her eye caught a flash of motion from the audience.

Hey, Peace is walking out! she realized. Why wasn't Stephanie stopping her? Peace needed to be watching this—or she'd never be able to get the number right.

"Michelle, what are you—" Stephanie exclaimed.

Bam!

Michelle crashed into the piano at the edge of the stage. Mr. Lang stopped playing. Everyone stared at Michelle as she hopped around on one foot, holding her ankle.

"Ow! Ow! Ow! Ow!" she yelped with each hop.

"Are you okay?" Mandy cried.

"Not really," Michelle answered. "My ankle is killing me."

"Why don't you go sit down until it feels better?" Stephanie suggested.

Michelle nodded. She limped to the steps, climbed down, and returned to her seat in the front row.

"Well, that one definitely wasn't perfect. Let's start again," Stephanie said. She gave Mr. Lang the signal, and everyone launched into the number from the beginning.

Minus Michelle.

Michelle leaned over and rubbed her ankle. It was already feeling a little better. She rubbed a little harder, then rolled her foot from side to side.

Her toes knocked into Peace's backpack, and it gaped open. Michelle could see, peeking out of the bag, a script, and a cosmetics bag, and—

She gasped. And a pair of dancing shoes!

Peace said she didn't have her dancing shoes. And there was no way she could have missed them when she looked in her backpack. They took up practically the whole bag.

What was going on?

Michelle didn't know. But she was definitely going to find out. Right now!

She stood up and crept down the aisle. Every second she expected to hear Stephanie yell at her, asking where she was going. But she made it out of the auditorium without getting caught.

Now all she had to do was find Peace. The lobby was empty, so the girls' room seemed the next logical place to try.

Michelle hurried over, ignoring the slight soreness in her ankle. She reached for the door—then froze. Someone inside was singing "Hopelessly Devoted to You."

It had to be Peace. "Hopelessly Devoted" was one of Sandy's big songs.

Michelle pressed her ear against the door. The singing was beautiful!

Peace is really good, she thought. Wait a minute, though. If Peace was singing this well, why did she say she had laryngitis?

This situation was getting weirder and weirder.

She decided the best thing to do was just ask Peace what was going on. Stephanie obviously wasn't going to.

Michelle pulled open the door. Hey! It wasn't Peace singing at all. It was Anna Abdul from Michelle's class! Anna wasn't even performing in the show. She was just there to paint sets.

"You sounded great, Anna!" Michelle exclaimed. "Why didn't you sign up to be in the show? We could really use you out there!"

Anna shook her head. "I sing only when I'm alone. In front of people my throat gets all tight. I can't sing a note."

"Maybe you could—" Michelle began.

"I—umm—I have to get back to work on the sets," Anna said. Michelle noticed that her face was beginning to turn red. She slipped past Michelle. "Bye," she said over her shoulder.

"Anna, have you seen Peace?" Michelle called after her.

Anna stopped and turned around. "She went outside a couple of minutes ago."

"Thanks." Michelle headed outside. She really needed to talk to Peace. The whole show could turn out to be a disaster if Peace didn't start rehearsing soon.

Michelle spotted a couple of kids sitting on the lawn outside the auditorium. Both kids were staring at something to one side of the building. Michelle had a feeling she knew exactly what they were looking at—the big teen star Peace Smith.

Michelle hurried along the side of the large red brick building. She neared the corner and heard a murmuring sound.

Michelle took a peek and saw Peace standing a few yards away. She was holding a cell phone to her ear.

"I don't know if that would be such a good idea," Peace said into the phone.

Her voice was clear and firm.

With no trace of laryngitis!

She lied to us! Michelle thought. *About the laryngitis* and *about not having the shoes.*

Michelle wanted to race up to her and demand to know what was going on.

But what if Peace just lied again?

No, Michelle needed to come up with another way to find out the truth. She would, too—no matter what it took!

Chapter 11

Stephanie walked into the kitchen. "Can I talk to you for a minute, Dad?" she asked Danny.

Stephanie realized she really needed his advice, and this was the perfect time to get it. Michelle was already in bed. Uncle Jesse and Aunt Becky were upstairs. D.J. was studying with a friend. And Joey was out doing one of his comedy shows.

Danny looked up from the notes he was making for *Wake Up, San Francisco!* the next morning.

"Of course, honey," he answered.

Stephanie sat down at the table. She had

to find just the right way of saying what she wanted to say. After all, Michelle was one of Danny's daughters, too. She gave the lazy Susan in the middle of the table a spin.

"I have a problem," she finally admitted.

Her father frowned. "Are you sick? Is it something at school? Are you—"

"It's Michelle," Stephanie interrupted softly. "I don't know what to do about her."

Danny leaned back in his chair. "I thought you two had been getting along lately," he said. "You've been spending all that time together working on the show."

He was getting that disappointed-Dad sound in his voice. It always made Stephanie feel guilty.

This time, though, she didn't have anything to feel guilty about, she told herself. Michelle—that's who should be feeling guilty. She was being a total pain.

"I *have* been working a ton on the show," Stephanie agreed. "And I think it's coming along great. But all Michelle does is complain. Every rehearsal, there's something she doesn't like. Or something she thinks I'm doing wrong. She never lets up! What do I do to get her to stop?"

Danny rose from his seat. "Uhhh—I'm going to have some ice cream. You want some?" he asked.

"You're stalling, Dad," Stephanie remarked.

He laughed. "You're right. I am stalling. I like to think I always have the right answer to whatever problems you girls are having, but I don't. Sometimes, I need to think about it for a little while. Ice cream usually helps the thinking process."

He grabbed two bowls out of the cupboard over the sink. Then he headed to the freezer and peered inside. "Rocky Road?" he asked.

"Two scoops," Stephanie answered.

"Michelle's usually so enthusiastic about everything," Danny said as he dished out the ice cream. "And I know she was really excited about this show. It's strange that she'd be difficult about this."

Her dad set a bowl and spoon in front of her, then he sat back down beside her. "What do *you* think is going on with her?" he asked. He spooned a bite of ice cream into his mouth.

Stephanie smiled to herself. *That's a favorite*

Dad technique, she thought. *You ask him for advice and then he tries to make you give advice to yourself!*

Stephanie sighed. "I don't know. She's driving me crazy, but she does want the show to be a success, because she wants to earn money for Samantha's operation—I'm sure of that. I mean, the show was her idea in the first place."

"That could be the problem," Danny said. "It was her idea, and now, suddenly, it's *your* show. At least that's how it seems to an outsider."

"But Michelle isn't old enough to handle a big show," Stephanie exclaimed. "And once Peace agreed to be in the show, the show got very *big*."

Her dad raised one eyebrow and took another spoonful of ice cream. He didn't look exactly convinced.

Stephanie stirred her ice cream into a lumpy soup. "Dad, I'm really the only one who understands Peace. We're becoming friends again, so she trusts me to help her 'develop her character' and everything. Can you see Michelle talking to Peace about motivation and stuff?"

"Probably not," Danny admitted. "But that's only one small part of putting on a show. Are you really telling me that there's *nothing* Michelle could handle?"

Stephanie stared into her dish. "I guess I could let her do a little more than I have," she mumbled.

"You know, I think that's all it would take to make her happy," Danny said. He swallowed a spoonful of ice cream. "Remember when you were little and you wanted to make a cake for my birthday?"

Stephanie felt a burst of anger go through her even though the cake incident had happened years and years ago. "Yeah, D.J. totally took over! I wanted to make a cake shaped like a turtle and she told me it was dumb!"

Stephanie stopped short. "It's the same thing, isn't it?" she realized.

"Keep that in mind when you start getting frustrated with Michelle," Danny advised.

"I will," Stephanie answered. "And I'm sure things will get a lot better between us. I'm her big sister. Working things out with Michelle is part of my job description!"

Chapter
12

"I shouldn't be here," Mandy told Michelle that Saturday morning. "I still haven't gotten my part in the first number down pat. I should be working on it, not hanging out at the mall."

"And I should be doing some homework," Cassie said. "I barely started my book report. I don't have time to be goofing around."

"We're not goofing around," Michelle told them. "We're on a mission . . . to save our show from total disaster!"

"I don't get it. How is spying on Peace going to save the show?" Mandy asked.

"I don't even get why the show might be a

total disaster in the first place," Cassie said. "Well, except if Mandy doesn't figure out which one is her left foot," she joked.

Mandy moaned. "I think I have *two* left feet."

"Listen, guys," Michelle told them. "There's something strange going on with Peace. It's something that's keeping her from joining in at the rehearsals. And we have to find out what it is."

She grabbed Cassie's arm with one hand and Mandy's arm with the other. She pulled them down the main walkway of the lower level of the mall.

"We have one hour before we have to meet my uncle Jesse again. Peace is in the mall somewhere—I heard Stephanie talking to her on the phone, telling her it was the only good place to shop and that she should hit the stores before rehearsal," Michelle explained. "Our job is to find her."

"And then what?" Cassie asked.

"And then . . . and then I'll put my plan into action!" Michelle said firmly.

Not that I actually have a plan, Michelle thought. She didn't want Cassie and Mandy to know that, though. If they did, they'd totally freak.

"There she is!" Mandy exclaimed. "Coming out of Bath and Bubbles."

"It looks like she bought half the store. Look at the size of that bag," Cassie said.

"Don't let her see us," Michelle ordered. She ducked behind one of the potted palm trees, dragging Cassie and Mandy down with her.

"Would you please stop pulling me?" Cassie asked. She jerked her arm free of Michelle's grip.

"Okay, she's far enough away for us to follow without her spotting us," Michelle said. "Let's go."

She moved out from behind the palm and strolled after Peace. She stayed just close enough to keep her in sight.

"I think she's heading toward Marjorie's," Mandy said.

That made sense. Marjorie's was one of the nicest stores in the mall. It was exactly the kind of place where someone like Peace would shop.

"Yep, she's going in," Cassie said.

"We're going in after her," Michelle told them. "But first we put on these." She handed each of her friends a pair of large sunglasses with super-dark lenses. Then she put on a pair of the shades herself.

"I can hardly see!" Cassie complained. "I'm not going to be able to tell which person is Peace."

"You'll get used to them," Michelle answered. "And we can't just walk in without some kind of disguise."

Mandy took a step toward the door.

"Wait! Not yet!" Michelle said. She peered into the store window. The salesgirl was holding up a couple of dresses for Peace. Peace smiled and nodded.

"What's happening?" Mandy whispered. "Is Peace trading top secret info about our show with a salesgirl spy?"

"Very funny," Michelle said. She kept her eyes locked on Peace. Peace took one of the dresses and headed to the dressing rooms.

"This is it!" Michelle cried. "Move, move, move!" She rushed into the store with Cassie and Mandy trailing behind her.

"Can I help you girls?" the salesgirl asked politely.

"I, um, want to try this on," Michelle answered, pulling the first shirt she saw off the rack next to her. It was neon green with hot-pink stripes, and the material felt like plastic.

"Ugh," Cassie said. "That shirt looks like this tablecloth my mom used to have. It melted in the sun during a picnic."

Michelle grabbed two more of the shirts off the rack and shoved them in Cassie's and Mandy's hands. "They want to try on the shirt, too," she said to the salesgirl, using her sweetest voice.

I have to get into one of those dressing rooms before Peace comes out and sees us, Michelle thought.

"Go on back," the salesgirl said. She pointed toward the fitting rooms.

"Thanks!" Michelle called. She herded Cassie and Mandy past the velvet curtain that separated the dressing rooms from the rest of the store. "Let's all go in one room," she whispered.

"That one's empty," Mandy noticed.

"*All* of them are empty—except that one," Cassie pointed out.

"So we know that's where Peace is," Michelle whispered.

"Yeah, I can see her Bath and Bubbles bag sticking out from under the door," Mandy added, her voice so low, Michelle could hardly hear it.

Michelle opened the door of the room across from Peace's and Cassie and Mandy reluctantly stepped inside. Michelle shut the door behind them.

"This feels wrong, Michelle," Mandy whispered. "We're going too far."

"I don't think Peace would be happy if she knew we followed her in here," Cassie agreed.

"We're not doing anything except trying on some clothes," Michelle whispered back. Mandy held the shirt up in front of her and studied herself in the mirror. "Ohhhh, these colors are making me nauseous," she said.

Michelle held her finger up to her lips, reminding her friends to keep their voices down.

"Wait a minute," Cassie whispered. "What's that noise?"

"Yeah," Mandy said. "What *is* that?"

"It sounds like—singing," Michelle responded. "Sort of." She listened hard to the noise coming from the fitting room across from theirs. Yes, it was definitely singing. She could make out the words now.

"Hooopelesssly deeevoted to youuuu!"

The high note made Michelle's teeth ache. It was more like a screech than any kind of song.

"That's Peace!" Michelle whispered. "She's singing one of the songs from the show!"

Mandy's eyes widened. "It can't be Peace! That person has the worst voice I've ever heard!"

"We're the only ones back here. It's not any of the three of us singing. So it *has* to be Peace," Michelle answered.

"I suddenly think I understand why the show could be a disaster," Cassie said.

"Yeah, Peace hasn't wanted to rehearse because she can't sing," Michelle said. "She probably can't dance, either!"

"What are we going to do now?" Mandy wailed. The singing was more than loud enough to drown out her voice.

Michelle swallowed hard. "There's only one thing to do," she whispered. "We have to kick Peace out of the show."

*   *   *

"Stephanie, before we leave for rehearsal, there's something I need to talk to you about," Michelle said that afternoon.

"Good. Because there's something I need to talk to you about, too," Stephanie answered. She patted the spot next to her on her bed. Michelle sat down beside her.

I'm not going to say I told you so or anything mean, Michelle promised herself. *Stephanie had no way of knowing that Peace stinks.*

She took a deep breath. "Steph, I found out that—" she began.

"Wait, let me go first," Stephanie interrupted.

Michelle slapped her hand down on Stephanie's pillow. "You never let me finish anything I'm trying to say," she complained.

"It's just that I know what I'm going to tell you is going to make you really happy," Stephanie said.

"Listen. I realize that I haven't been very fair to you," she explained. "You came up with the idea for the show, and then I got Peace involved and completely took it over."

Michelle stared at her sister. Wow! She never expected her to say anything like that!

"At rehearsal this afternoon I think we should divide the cast into two groups," Stephanie suggested. "I'll work on the Sandra Dee song with Peace and the girls. And you can work on "Greased Lightning" with the guys. Most of them still have no clue about the steps, and you're great at all the dances in the show. I know you can teach them what to do."

"Sure, that would be excellent!" Michelle answered. She'd been dying for a chance to whip that number into shape.

She smoothed out Stephanie's pillow. "But, Steph, that's not exactly what I wanted to talk to you about. See, I found out that—"

"Wait! I almost forgot!" Stephanie exclaimed. "There's something else. I got you a present."

She jumped up, pulled open her dresser drawer, and took out a baseball cap. "For you," she said. She tossed it to Michelle.

Michelle grinned as she saw the word stitched across the front: Co-director.

"I got one for me, too," Stephanie said. She reached into the drawer and pulled out a hat identical to Michelle's.

Identical. It said Co-director, too.

Not director. Co-director.

This was great! This meant Stephanie was finally ready to be Michelle's partner—instead of her boss.

"This is great, Stephanie," Michelle said. "Thanks!"

"So, now, *co-director*, what was it that you wanted to talk to me about?" Stephanie asked.

"Right. Well, like I was saying, *co-director*, we have a problem," Michelle stated. "I found out that Peace—"

"Oh, I forgot. I wanted to talk to you about Peace, too. You should probably just let me worry about her, okay?" Stephanie said. "I think that it will work best if we both have separate parts of the show to handle. Peace feels more comfortable around me, so I'll deal with everything involving her."

Stephanie moved toward the door. "Well, I've got to call the printer and check up on the programs before we go. See you later." She started for the door, then hesitated, and turned back to Michelle. "Unless you want to do it?"

"No, it's fine. You can do it," Michelle answered. "But I really need to talk about Peace."

Let's Put On a Show

"Michelle, I meant what I said," Stephanie stated. "I'm handling everything involving Peace. You don't have to worry about her at all."

She walked out of the room and shut the door behind her.

Chapter
13

That streak right there, between those two clouds, is my favorite color of pink," Michelle told her father that evening.

Danny and Michelle were strolling through the hills of their neighborhood as the sun set in front of them.

"It's like the inside of a seashell," her dad commented.

"Yeah. Exactly," Michelle answered. "And that darker patch, it's like the cherry taffy they sell at the snack shack by the baseball field."

She had asked her dad to go for a walk after dinner because she wanted to talk to him—

but not about all the colors of pink in the sunset.

About Stephanie.

Somehow, though, she didn't know how to start. It was like all the things she wanted to say were stuck somewhere under her rib cage, and the words weren't close to coming out of her mouth.

"You ready to head back?" Danny asked. "Or should we go a little farther?"

"Farther," Michelle said quickly.

Her dad took her hand as they crossed the street. That was something he hadn't done since she was really little. Michelle had to admit that it was kind of nice. Especially when she had a problem on her mind.

"Is something bothering you?" he asked. "I noticed you ate only half a taco tonight, and I made your favorite kind."

That one question jarred loose all the words trapped in Michelle's chest.

"Stephanie is driving me insane!" she burst out. "She never listens to me—never! I've been trying to tell her something really important, and she keeps ignoring me. And all because she's the big sister and I'm the little sister, so she thinks she knows better about *everything!*"

"So—this is about your show," Danny guessed.

"There's not going to be a show if Steph doesn't listen to me. Or there will only be a show that no one wants to see. A total disaster of a show."

Michelle's words came out so fast, they tumbled over one another. She took a deep breath and tried to slow down a little.

"Dad, would you please talk to Stephanie for me?" Michelle begged. "If *you* tell her to pay attention to me, she'll *have* to listen."

Danny laughed. "I don't think it's that easy."

"But it is," Michelle insisted.

Her dad gave her hand a squeeze. "You know that's not the way we do things, Michelle. I want you and Stephanie to work this out for yourselves."

Michelle sighed. Her father always wanted them to work out problems on their own. He said it was all part of growing up.

"I don't see how we can," Michelle complained. "Especially when she won't even listen to me!"

"Maybe you need to choose a better time and place for a conversation," Danny suggested. "Don't try talking in the middle of a rehearsal, when a hundred things are going on at once."

"You mean, I should talk to her in our bedroom or something, when it's just the two of us?" Michelle asked.

"You've got it," he answered.

"Tried that," Michelle reported. "It didn't work."

"Oh. Well. I guess we need a plan B," Danny said. He thought for a moment. "How about writing down what you want to tell her? That way, Stephanie can read it by herself and have time to think about what you're saying."

"Yeah! And she wouldn't be able to interrupt a letter," Michelle stated.

She felt her steps get a little bouncier. Her dad's idea might really work.

"Let's turn around now," she suggested. "I have some writing to do."

"Steph, did you get a chance to read the note I left on your dresser?" Michelle asked.

The two girls rushed toward the auditorium for the Sunday afternoon rehearsal. They each wore their Co-director hats. Stephanie said it made them look totally professional.

"Um, no, not yet," Stephanie mumbled. She was flipping through the lists on her clipboard as she walked. "Today I want everyone to work on 'Summer Nights' first, if that's okay with you, Michelle. Then I want you to work with the guys again. You did a great job with them yesterday."

"Fine," Michelle answered. "But I really need you to read the—"

"Oh, there's your friend Karlee!" Stephanie exclaimed. "I want to let her know what a great job she's been doing selling tickets! She's sold the most of anyone so far!"

Stephanie rushed off before Michelle could say another word. *At this rate, I don't think Dad's plan B is going to work*, she thought.

She spotted Mandy and Cassie by the big double doors. They were obviously waiting for her. And they looked as worried as Michelle felt.

"So did you try to talk to Stephanie again?" Cassie demanded.

"Is Stephanie going to fire Peace?" Mandy jumped in.

"Come on! Tell us!" Cassie cried.

"I wrote her a note about what we saw— and heard, but she hasn't read it yet," Michelle admitted. "I don't know if she ever will."

"Maybe you should hire a plane to write your note in the sky," Cassie said. It sounded like a joke, but Michelle noticed that her friend wasn't smiling.

"Or maybe you could send a singing telegram," Mandy suggested. She wasn't smiling, either.

"That would work if Peace did the singing," Michelle answered. "Then Stephanie would have to accept how completely bad Peace is."

"Maybe Mandy and I could talk to her," Cassie said. "We were eye—I mean ear—witnesses!"

Michelle shook her head. "No, it wouldn't work," she said. "I'm pretty sure Stephanie thinks I don't know what I'm talking about because I'm a little kid. And since you guys are the same age as me—"

"She thinks of us as little kids, too," Mandy finished.

"Bingo," Michelle told her.

"Hey, come on inside, you three!" Michelle heard Stephanie call. She glanced over her shoulder and saw her older sister rushing toward them.

"Peace will be here in a few minutes," Stephanie said when she reached them. "I want all the cast in their opening places when she arrives so we can go right into rehearsing. I can't wait to see the number *with* our Sandy."

"You mean Peace is going to rehearse with us today—and not just watch?" Cassie asked.

Stephanie grinned. "That's right. I talked to her this morning, and her laryngitis is gone!"

She pushed open one of the auditorium doors and waved Michelle, Cassie, and Mandy inside.

"Looks like Stephanie's going to get her singing telegram after all," Mandy whispered in Michelle's ear as they headed through the lobby.

Michelle felt a twinge of pity for Stephanie. It was going to be so embarrassing for her when Peace opened her mouth and those horrible *sounds* started coming out.

At least once Stephanie heard Peace sing,

Michelle's problem would be solved. There was no way Stephanie would let Peace keep the lead in the show after rehearsal.

Michelle dropped her backpack in the first row of seats, then climbed up onstage. She felt the muscles in her neck and shoulders relax a little.

Everything's going to be okay, she told herself. *After Stephanie realizes that there's no way Peace can be our Sandy, I'll convince her that Anna Abdul would be perfect for the part. We'll recast the role, and the show will be great!*

After the truth came out, Stephanie would realize that she should have been listening to Michelle all along.

"Okay, everyone," Stephanie called. "Places for the first number. Places! Peace will be here any minute."

Michelle obediently sat down on one end of the long table on stage right.

"I guess I better make sure I'm ready for my first performance with my gorgeous co-star," Eli announced. He pulled out a little canister of breath spray and shot a double dose into his mouth.

Mandy caught Michelle's eye, then stuck

her finger in her mouth and pretended to gag.

A faint ringing sound met Michelle's ears.

"Is that the phone in the lobby?" Darcy called from her spot on the other side of the table. "I gave that number to the minister at my church. He's arranging to bring our whole youth group to the show!"

She jumped off the table and hurried off-stage and out of the auditorium. "I'll be right back," she called.

"Okay, everyone. Remember that in this number you're all dying to find out about Danny and Sandy's summer romance. Don't just sing the words. *Feel* the words," Stephanie coached. "This will be your first time performing with Peace, and—"

"Peace isn't coming," Darcy called from the back of the auditorium.

"What?" Stephanie cried.

"She said that she has to audition for a shampoo commercial," Darcy replied as she headed toward them. "And this is the only time that the casting people could see her."

Stephanie sighed. "I guess this is just part of the price we have to pay for having a big star in our show," she said. "Okay, everyone. Let's go ahead and rehearse the number without her."

No way, Michelle thought. *Absolutely no way!*

If this keeps going, the first time Steph will hear Peace sing is on opening night.

Right before we all get booed off the stage!

Michelle pushed herself to her feet and stood on top of the table.

If the only way to get Stephanie to listen is to stand up here and shout, she thought, *I'm going to do it!*

STEPHANIE

Chapter
14

Hold on, everyone. Before we start the number, we're going to have auditions for the part of Sandy! Peace Smith needs to be replaced!" Michelle shouted from the top of the stage-right table. Her hands were planted on her hips, and she was staring directly at Stephanie.

"Michelle, what are you talking about? Get down from there!" Stephanie ordered.

"I'm co-director, remember?" Michelle pointed to the words stitched across the front of her baseball cap. "And I'm not going to let *my* show get ruined by Peace Smith! We need a new Sandy. Now!"

Stephanie couldn't believe this. Michelle had totally lost it.

"Get down, and we'll talk about this in private," Stephanie said.

Everyone in the cast was hanging on every word. They kept turning their heads from Stephanie to Michelle as if they were watching the ball at a tennis match.

"No," Michelle answered, her voice loud and strong. "It's too late for that. Besides, I want everyone to hear this. It's their show, too."

Clearly, talking to Michelle wasn't going to get Stephanie anywhere. She turned her attention to the cast.

"Look, everyone, I know it's been hard rehearsing without Peace. But we have to remember that she's doing us a favor by being in our show. I mean, she's been on television and everything."

"And she's a babe," one of the guys yelled.

"We *need* Peace," Stephanie continued. "Almost everyone who bought a ticket is coming to see *her*. And she's going to be fantastic. I promise you that!"

"You're wrong!" Michelle shot back. "I

heard Peace sing—and she's terrible. Not just a little bad. She's terr-i-ble!"

For a moment, Stephanie wondered if Michelle could be right. It *was* kind of weird that Peace hadn't practiced even once.

She shook her head. *No way*, she decided. *Peace is a star. And you have to be super-talented to be a star.*

Stephanie crossed her arms over her chest. "Michelle, you are being so incredibly selfish. Obviously, you're still mad that I took over organizing the show. You wanted to be the director, star, choreographer, and everything else. And since that didn't happen, you're acting like a big baby."

Mandy climbed up on the table next to Michelle. "I heard Peace, too," she told the group. "Michelle's right. She doesn't even sound human when she sings. She sounds like a sick seal."

Cassie joined Michelle and Mandy. "If Peace is in this show, it's going to be a total disaster. We'll have to hand out earplugs at the door!"

"What's the deal here, Steph?" her friend Marco called out. "Do these kids know what they're talking about?"

Let's Put On a Show

"The deal is this," Stephanie said. "We're putting on a show to raise money for Samantha O'Reilly, and Peace Smith generously offered to help us. Even if she's not a perfect singer—and I still don't know that that's true—with her as the star of our show, we're going to be able to bring in a lot of money. We need that money to get Samantha her operation!"

Stephanie glanced over at Michelle. "You didn't forget about Samantha, did you?" she challenged her sister.

Michelle jerked up her chin. "Of course I didn't forget about Samantha. Samantha's my friend. But a show starring Peace isn't going to make any money—because everyone will be asking for a refund when they hear her sing!"

All right, this conversation has gone far enough, Stephanie thought. She clapped her hands. "Let's not waste any more time on this. Everyone, our first show is Friday night! The only part I want any of you thinking about right now is your own—not Peace's!"

Michelle jumped off the table and marched

straight over to Stephanie. "I just have one more thing to say to you," she announced.

The auditorium grew so quiet that Stephanie could hear people breathing.

"Fine. Then say it and get it over with," Stephanie snapped.

"Either Peace goes—or I go!" Michelle announced. "I'll just do my own show."

"You're being ridiculous!" Stephanie exclaimed. "There's no way you're going to be able to come up with a whole new show and be ready to perform it in time."

"We aren't going to come up with a whole new show," Michelle answered. "This show isn't just yours. It's mine, too. It's all of ours. We're going to put on *Grease* in the auditorium of *my* school!"

Stephanie felt as if she'd been punched in the stomach. "I don't think anyone is going to come to see you, Cassie, and Mandy try to do an entire show by yourselves."

"They won't be by themselves," Michelle's friend Jeff yelled. He swung himself off the stage and joined the group of deserters.

Stephanie watched in shock as almost every one of the kids from Michelle's school stampeded off the stage. That was half her cast! She felt anger flooding through her. She couldn't control it anymore.

"Go ahead and leave!" Stephanie shouted. "We don't need any of you to put on a great show. We have Peace Smith!"

"Don't worry, everything is totally under control," Stephanie told Allie and Darcy as they headed to rehearsal after school on Monday. "To tell you the truth, I think we're better off without Michelle and her friends in the show."

"I'm not so sure, Stephanie," Allie pointed out. "They really did put their all into every number. We're going to lose a lot of energy without them."

"Umm—do you think we're better off without our *sets* in the show?" Darcy cried. "Because there they go!" She pointed toward the auditorium.

Stephanie gasped. Michelle and her friends were carrying out the set with the racing car painted on it. No. No way! Stephanie's group couldn't do the "Greased Lightning" number without that set! The whole song was about the car!

"Put that back! Right now!" Stephanie yelled. She raced up to Michelle and her group and blocked their way.

"We're not taking all the sets," Michelle said. "Just half. That's only fair. My friends did as much work on them as your friends. More, even. Anna Abdul painted the whole car on this one."

"Umm, Steph. That's true," Allie mumbled.

"I guess you have to let Michelle have some of them," Darcy agreed.

Stephanie stepped out of the way. She headed into the auditorium without another word to Michelle. There was nothing she had to say to her.

In fact, just then, she felt as if she didn't want to talk to her again—ever!

"So, I'm going to walk Allie through some of the dance numbers before everyone else shows up," Darcy said.

"I don't know how well I'm going to do as a replacement for Michelle. She's a lot better dancer than I am," Allie said. "And I have only four days to rehearse!"

"Everybody is going to be watching Peace anyway," Stephanie snapped. "The audience wouldn't notice if you dyed your hair purple and crawled across the stage on all fours!"

"Oh, that makes me feel so much better," Allie answered. She sounded hurt.

"Sorry," Stephanie told her, feeling guilty. "I'm just—"

"I know," Allie said. "It's okay."

Stephanie sighed. "I guess I better go backstage and inventory the sets. I'll make a list of what we need to replace."

"Everyone will pitch in to get it done," Darcy told her. "Don't stress."

Don't stress? Stephanie thought. Opening night was only four days away! How could she not stress?

Stephanie climbed the stairs to the stage and trudged around to the big open space where the sets were stored. Peace was sitting on one of the tables for the "Summer Nights" number.

"Hi! You're early!" Stephanie exclaimed.

"Yeah. But I have to leave in a minute," Peace blurted out. "I have another audition."

Okay. I've been understanding enough, Stephanie thought. *I have to find a way to tell*

Peace that she needs to show everyone that the show is important to her.

But how can I say that to Peace Smith? she wondered. *She's a star! And I'm just . . . Stephanie.*

She took a deep breath. That didn't matter, she decided. She had to try.

Stephanie walked over and sat down next to Peace. *Just say it*, she ordered herself. *You have to.*

"Our show is in four days and you haven't actually rehearsed even once," she told Peace.

"I know. You're right," Peace said. She pulled at a loose thread in her long skirt. It made an ugly snag. "Oh, Steph, I've messed up so badly! I don't think I can be in the show at all!"

Stephanie's heart froze in her chest. Then it started beating triple time.

Was Peace quitting the show?

"Why? What do you mean?" she exclaimed.

"I didn't know that you wanted me to be in a musical when I said yes," Peace rushed on. "I've never done any professional singing or dancing. And . . . and . . ."

"And you're nervous," Stephanie finished for her.

"Petrified," Peace corrected her.

Ah-ha! Stephanie thought. *Now I know why Peace wouldn't rehearse with us! It makes perfect sense! She was nervous! In fact, that was probably why she sounded so bad when Michelle heard her singing the other day!*

Wow. I didn't think anything could petrify a star. Stephanie smiled to herself, realizing how silly that was. Peace was just a girl, too. The same girl Stephanie had been with in the first grade.

"Remember how afraid you were of Nathan Frieder?" she asked Peace.

"I probably would have quit coming to school if it weren't for you and Allie," Peace said. "I was that scared. And then he turned out to be a big baby. Remember? He almost cried when he found that paste sandwich we put in his lunch box."

"But you might still be afraid of Nathan if you hadn't stood up to him. Right?" Stephanie said.

Peace started to pluck at another loose thread. Stephanie put a hand over Peace's to stop her.

"So what you're saying is that I have to

1 2 3

stand up to my fear of singing and dancing?" Peace asked.

Stephanie nodded. "Why don't you just sing a song for me right here, right now? No pressure or anything. No audience. Just you and me."

Peace had four days to get used to singing in front of people. And Stephanie knew she could do it. After all, Peace was a pro. It probably wouldn't take half that time for her to get comfortable with it.

"You want me to sing? Right here? Right now?" Peace repeated.

"Yeah. It will make you feel a whole lot better," Stephanie told her.

"You're right." Peace stood up and faced Stephanie. She took a few deep breaths, closed her eyes, and launched into her song "Hopelessly Devoted to You."

"Guuuess miiiine is nooot the fiiiirst heeeart broooken," she began.

Oh, no! That isn't singing! Stephanie thought. *It isn't even howling.*

A horrible thought hit Stephanie—Michelle was right!

Peace continued to sing. A moment later

Darcy and Allie appeared backstage. Stephanie was glad that Peace couldn't see their faces. They looked as horrified as she felt.

"Oh, no!" Darcy mouthed at Stephanie.

Stephanie shook her head and shrugged her shoulders. "Um—okay, Peace, that's fine. Just fine," she said.

Peace opened her eyes and smiled. "Really?"

"Let's try some dancing now," Stephanie said, avoiding the question. "Darcy, take Peace through one of the combinations, okay?"

Please let her be able to dance, Stephanie thought. *If she can dance, I can just make her singing solos group numbers—and work in a lot more dancing.*

"Why don't we start with a basic jazz diamond, just to get warmed up," Darcy suggested. She positioned herself next to Peace.

"You cross your left foot in front of your right. Then step back with your right," Darcy explained. She demonstrated as she spoke. "Then step to the side with your left. And then in front with your right."

"Got it," Peace said. "I step over with my right."

Peace picked up her right foot—and put it down on top of her left foot.

She teetered for a moment.

Then she stumbled into Darcy, and they both landed on the floor.

Peace looked like a tree toppling over in the forest, Stephanie thought. A beautiful tree, but still—a tree.

Stephanie rubbed her face with both hands.

Okay, she thought. *Peace can't sing.* And *she can't dance. That means—*

That means my show is completely ruined!

Chapter 15

Stephanie dropped her backpack on the kitchen table. She slumped into the closest chair and hung her head in her hands.

The show is ruined. The words pounded through her brain again. *The show is ruined. The show is ruined.*

"What am I going to do?" Stephanie whispered to herself.

According to her records, all three performances of the show were sold out. There was even a waiting list!

"Guess mine is not the first heart broken," a high, sweet voice began to sing.

Stephanie groaned. Michelle was playing the sound track to *Grease*!

She wanted to ask her to shut it off. If she did, it might start another fight, and she couldn't deal with that. Her day had been way, way too hideous already.

"Okay, now try it with the blindfold off!" Stephanie heard Michelle call from the backyard.

The song cut off in the middle.

It started up a moment later. But the voice sounded cracked and quivery.

Wait! What's going on? Stephanie thought.

She got up and hurried over to the kitchen window. She peeked around the edge of the curtain and saw Michelle and Anna Abdul standing in the middle of the yard. The rest of the kids who were doing the show with Michelle stood off to one side.

"Maybe she should try it with the blindfold again," Cassie suggested.

Michelle shook her head. "There's no time. The show is only three days away," she answered.

Stephanie studied Anna for a minute. Even from the kitchen Stephanie could tell how uncomfortable Anna was. Her arms were folded across her chest, and her shoulders were all hunched up.

"Anna, try it with your eyes half closed," Michelle instructed. "It will make everything kind of blurry. And remember, you're not Anna. You're Sandy."

Anna said something in reply, but her voice was too soft for Stephanie to hear. Then she narrowed her eyes into little slits, stood up straight, and started to sing.

No wonder I thought Michelle was playing a CD. Anna has a beautiful voice, Stephanie realized.

Stephanie stood frozen in place until Anna finished.

Michelle is right, she thought. *Anna is Sandy when she sings.*

"Great job!" Michelle exclaimed. "We'll keep working tomorrow, and by Friday night I know you're going to be singing loud and clear—and with your eyes wide open."

Anna gave an embarrassed smile as the whole group burst into a round of applause.

"Remember, we're having a work party at the school auditorium after dinner tonight,"

Michelle announced. "We have a bunch of sets to build. Bring your parents, bring your friends, bring your brothers and sisters. We need all the help we can get!"

Hey! Stephanie had another realization. Michelle was a pretty good director! Although, Stephanie and her friends had gotten the show organized faster than Michelle and her crew would have.

But Michelle was awesome out there— coaching Anna and pulling her whole show together.

"Hey, sweetie. Could I get some help unpacking these groceries?" Danny called as he headed into the kitchen.

"Sure," Stephanie answered. She walked over to him and took one of the brown paper bags out of his arms.

"Is that the one with the chips?" Danny asked. "I thought the troops out there could use a snack."

Stephanie pulled out two bags of chips and tossed them to her father. "Michelle's doing a good job," she said.

She hesitated. Then she blurted out what was really bothering her. "Her show is going to be a thousand times better than mine. I totally messed everything up! If I'd listened to Michelle . . ."

She shook her head, letting her words trail off.

"I heard all about it," Danny said. "And I think you might be talking to the wrong person." He poured the chips into a big wooden bowl and then held the bowl out to Stephanie.

She got the message. She had to make amends with Michelle.

"I guess you're right," she admitted. She took the bowl, lifted her head up high, and strode out the back door.

"Chips for everyone," she called as she hurried over to Michelle.

"Hey, thanks, Steph," Michelle said. She sounded surprised.

"Uh, I was wondering if I could talk to you—to all of you—for a minute?" Stephanie asked.

"We're pretty busy," Michelle answered. She took the bowl of chips and headed back toward her group.

"Yeah, *we* have a show to put on!" Mandy chimed in.

"I know, but it will take only a second. Please?" Stephanie said.

Michelle shrugged. Stephanie decided to take that as a yes.

"I wanted to tell all of you that I'm sorry," Stephanie said, speaking loud enough so everyone could hear. "Michelle was right. I shouldn't have asked Peace to be in the show without making her audition—or at least finding out if she could sing or dance. Because she can't do either—at all."

"So why did you do it?" Jeff called out.

"It's just that I knew Peace could bring in a lot of people, and that would earn more money for Samantha," she answered. "I figured that she's a star. And that stars must know how to do all those things. Boy, was I wrong."

Stephanie glanced from face to face. Some of the kids looked angry. Some looked sympathetic.

She checked Michelle's face. It was totally blank. Stephanie had no idea what her little sister was thinking.

"And that's not the only reason I asked Peace to be in the show," Stephanie admitted.

She decided she owed Michelle and the others the whole truth. "I wanted to have a chance to hang out with her. You know—to be friends with a real live celebrity."

Cassie and Mandy both nodded.

"I guess that's why I didn't get tough on her when she kept coming up with reasons not to rehearse." Stephanie was figuring out the whole thing as the words came out of her mouth. "I didn't want to do anything that would make Peace not like me."

Michelle continued to stare at Stephanie, her face showing no emotion.

"So, anyway, that's it," Stephanie told them. "I just wanted to say I'm sorry. And that Michelle was totally right."

Stephanie turned back toward the house.

She felt the teeny, tiniest bit better. Even if her show was going to be a laughingstock, at least she'd said what she needed to say.

"So what are you going to do now? About your show, I mean," Michelle asked.

Stephanie turned back to her sister. "I don't know," she admitted.

"Well, we really could use a bigger theater for *our* show," Michelle answered.

"And we could use some more dancers," Cassie said.

"And some more scenery," Mandy added.

"And some tickets," Lee jumped in.

"Do you think maybe you'd want to join our shows up again?" Michelle asked.

"Yes!" Stephanie exclaimed. "Yes! Yes! Yes!" She grabbed Michelle and twirled her around in a hug. "You're the best sister ever!"

A grin broke across Michelle's face, but it faded a moment later. "Steph, you know that you still have to ask Peace to leave the show, right?"

Stephanie nodded. She felt a dull weight settle in her stomach.

All her problems with the show were solved. Except one.

What in the world was she going to say to Peace?

555-6174. 555-6174. Okay. Stephanie had memorized Peace's phone number.

Now all she had to do was get up the guts to dial it. She had been sitting at her desk for almost fifteen minutes. Every minute or so, she reached for the phone, then pulled back her hand at the last second.

"Do it," Stephanie commanded herself. "You got yourself into this mess—now you have to get yourself out of it."

She reached for the phone again—and it rang.

Whew! Saved by the bell!

Stephanie hoped it was Darcy or Allie. If it was, she could ask them for advice about what to say to Peace.

She picked up the receiver. "Hello?"

"Hi, Stephanie!" a cheery voice greeted her. "It's Peace."

The phone slipped from Stephanie's hand. She caught it before it fell to the floor. "Oh . . . uh . . . hi!" Stephanie struggled to say. "Um, how's it going?"

"Great!" Peace exclaimed. "I really have to thank you, Steph. I was so afraid of dancing and singing in front of people. And you helped me get over it completely. Now I can't wait for opening night!"

"Actually, I was just about to call you to talk about the show," Stephanie said. "Uh—"

Stephanie fumbled for words but couldn't

think of anything to say that wouldn't make Peace feel horrible.

"What about the show?" Peace asked.

"The show is so small that I'm worried it will have a bad effect on your career," Stephanie blurted out. "You know, it might make you look like an amateur if you do a show in a school auditorium."

"No way!" Peace exclaimed. "The show is the perfect place for me to do my first musical. Plus, I really want to help Samantha."

She sounds so happy and excited, Stephanie thought. How am I supposed to tell her she's out?

"Oh, I've got another call," Peace said. "I'll see you at rehearsal tomorrow, okay?"

Stephanie swallowed hard. "Uh—okay. See you there."

Chapter
16

The show is going to be awesome," Michelle told Cassie and Mandy. They were walking from their school to the high school. There were only three days left until the premiere, but Michelle felt sure now that the show would be a hit.

"Are we going to keep the new ideas we came up with when we were working on our own?" Cassie asked.

"Definitely," Michelle answered.

"Did Stephanie say how Peace took the news that she couldn't be in the show?" Mandy questioned.

"Yeah. Is she feeling totally horrible?" Cassie added.

"I didn't get a chance to talk to her about it. She had to go run an errand with Aunt Becky last night. And then this morning she was out of the house while I was still brushing my teeth."

Mandy brushed her hair out of her eyes. "Maybe Peace is relieved," she said. "I would be if I were her. I mean, she must know she's a terrible singer and that it would be totally humiliating for her to be in the show."

"Maybe," Michelle answered. "But maybe not. Anna didn't know what a great singer she was, so maybe Peace didn't know she was awful."

Michelle didn't know which was worse— getting kicked out of the show and understanding the reason, or getting kicked out of the show and *not* understanding the reason.

Poor Peace!

Michelle felt really bad for her, especially because she was always so nice. But Michelle and Stephanie had no choice but to get rid of her. They had to think of the show—and Samantha—first.

"Just think, Friday night we'll be doing our opening night performance here," Mandy said when they reached the high school auditorium.

"I can't wait!" Cassie opened the door and led the way across the lobby.

"Hi, everyone!" Michelle cried as they burst through the lobby doors. "We're back!"

She felt a sharp elbow in her side. "Uh, Michelle, someone else is back, too," Mandy said through clenched teeth. "Someone we weren't expecting to see."

Michelle stopped and scanned the auditorium.

No!

She had to be seeing things.

She blinked once. Twice.

But it wasn't her imagination.

Peace Smith was sitting in the front row of the auditorium.

"I can't believe this!" Michelle yelped.

"Maybe there's an explanation," Cassie suggested. "Like maybe Peace became a really awesome singer overnight and came by to beg Stephanie for her spot back."

"Or maybe she got a great part in a movie and she stopped by to tell all of us about it," Mandy added.

"Then why is she climbing onstage?" Michelle demanded. "Why is she wearing her

Sandy costume? And why is that horrible sound coming out of her mouth?"

A wave of heat swept from the roots of Michelle's hair to her toes. "I'll tell you why," she said, answering her own question. "Because Stephanie lied to me!"

She spun around, bolted through the lobby door—and crashed straight into Stephanie!

"Hi, Michelle! I thought I'd get here before you!" Stephanie exclaimed.

"Hi—and good-bye," Michelle said.

"No, wait! We have to talk." Stephanie took her by the arm and led her over to the bench in the far corner of the lobby.

"What's the point of talking?" Michelle asked. "You're probably just going to lie to me again. Just like you did when you said you'd get rid of Peace!"

"First of all, I didn't lie. You have to believe me," Stephanie begged. She held on tight to Michelle's arm so she couldn't leave. "I tried to tell Peace she was out of the show. I really did!"

Stephanie sounds really upset, Michelle thought. *About as upset as I feel. Maybe I should give her a chance.*

"So what happened?" she asked.

"When I talked to Peace on the phone, she thanked me for helping her get over her fear of singing and dancing for an audience. Then she told me how excited she was to be in the show. She was just so grateful and excited—" Stephanie shrugged helplessly.

Michelle had to admit that she understood. Telling a friend bad news ranked right up there with going to the dentist.

Being the director of a show meant doing not-fun things, though. It was just part of the job.

"Why don't I go get her and bring her out here?" Michelle suggested. "We can tell her together if you want. But we have to do it, Steph. If we don't—"

"I know," Stephanie groaned. "Total disaster."

The front door of the auditorium swung open and two teenage guys peered in.

"Can I help you guys?" Stephanie asked.

The boys looked at each other. "He has something to give Peace," the taller guy said, pointing to his friend.

"No, *he* has something to give her," the shorter guy protested.

"You can't go in right now," Stephanie said. "There's a rehearsal going on."

"Okay," the tall guy said. "Well, can you just give her this?" He pulled a heart-shaped box of candy out of his backpack and put it on the bench next to the door.

"Give her this, too," the other guy said. He pulled a bunch of slightly wilted roses out from behind his back and dropped them next to the candy.

"Sure," Michelle said. "Do you want us to say who they're from?"

"No, uh, it's okay," the taller guy answered. "There's a card with them. We're just really big fans."

The two guys hurried away.

"Did you see how nervous they were?" Stephanie asked.

"Yeah," Michelle said. "They seemed really stuck on Peace!"

Stephanie sighed. "*That* is exactly our problem."

Michelle scrunched her eyebrows together. "Huh?"

"People love Peace," she answered. "People bought tickets to our show so that they could see Peace."

"But they'll leave if they hear her sing or see her dance," Michelle reminded her.

She crossed her fingers, hoping Stephanie wasn't going to try to weasel out of telling Peace she couldn't be in the show. If she did, Michelle was going to have to round up all her friends so they could start working on their own show again.

"Maybe people will leave if they don't see Peace at all," Stephanie answered. "Don't get me wrong, Anna's great, but do you think those two guys would care how great she is?"

Michelle glanced over at the flowers and candy. "I guess not," she admitted. "As Dad would say, I guess we need a plan B."

"Except at this point, it's more like a plan Z," Stephanie said.

"Do you really think we can come up with a way to keep Peace in the show without—" Michelle started.

"Without passing out blindfolds and earplugs?" Stephanie finished for her.

Michelle nodded.

"Well, there's something else Dad says," Stephanie began.

Michelle grinned. "I know! Two Tanner heads are better than one!"

"Exactly," Stephanie said. "So let's get to work."

Chapter
17

"Two minutes to show time, everybody!" Stephanie called.

She pulled the thick velvet curtain aside a fraction of an inch. She peeked into the audience. It was packed. Every single seat was filled.

She smiled as she spotted her whole family in the front row. Her dad, Joey, and Aunt Becky each had a video camera ready.

Michelle stepped up beside her and took a peek. "Samantha's definitely going to get one good video," she said.

"I hope the show is as good as the video coverage our family is giving us," Stephanie pointed out. Butterflies danced in her stomach. They'd had two days to put plan Z into effect. She hoped it would actually work.

"Full house?" Peace asked, coming up behind them.

"Completely full," Stephanie answered. She smiled at Peace. "You look absolutely fantastic."

"Amazing," Michelle agreed.

Peace was dressed in a long pink poodle skirt and white sweater. She had a pink kerchief tied around her neck. The color totally brought out Peace's rosy complexion and her amazing green eyes.

Peace practically glowed, Stephanie thought.

"I don't know about this, Michelle," Anna called. She stepped up next to Peace.

Anna tugged at the pink kerchief around her neck. Her outfit matched Peace's exactly. Perfect. Just like Stephanie and Michelle planned.

"Don't worry," Michelle told her friend. "You look great! And you're going to sound even better.

"Wish me—I mean *us*—luck," Peace said. She put an arm around Anna.

"You don't need luck," Stephanie assured her. "You're both totally ready."

"Thanks to you and Michelle," Peace said. "If you hadn't come up with this plan"—she gave a dramatic shiver—"I don't even want to think about it."

Stephanie glanced at her watch again. "Okay. We're on, Michelle." She smoothed her costume—a cheerleader outfit—then stepped through the curtain.

She and Michelle positioned themselves in front of the row of microphones that were hidden in the floor of the stage. An instant later the spotlights hit them.

"Ladies and gentlemen, welcome to our production of *Grease*," she said. She was relieved to hear her voice come out clear and strong.

"As you know, the proceeds from all our performances will go to the Samantha O'Reilly Fund," Michelle said.

"We want to thank Peace Smith for agreeing to take part in our play," Stephanie continued. "Most of all, we want to thank you for coming. Enjoy the show!"

Let's Put On a Show

Stephanie and Michelle walked offstage to a round of applause.

And the show began!

Halfway through now, Stephanie thought. I hope everyone likes it so far!

She glanced at the stage. Peace, as Sandy, sat in a backyard, in her flannel nightgown, crying because her boyfriend, Danny, had treated her badly. "What happened to the Danny I used to know?" she sniffed.

Stephanie gasped as she watched an actual tear run down Peace's cheek. The girl is good, she thought. Very good.

At that moment the music swelled. Peace froze in place, and Anna walked out onstage, wearing a nightgown that was totally identical to Peace's. She began to sing "Hopelessly Devoted to You," Sandy's song.

Michelle and Stephanie agreed that Peace should do all the acting as Sandy. But it was Michelle's idea to freeze the action—and have Anna step in as the "singing Sandy."

That way, Peace could still be Sandy, but didn't have to sing a note because Anna would perform all her songs!

They did the same with Danny's part. Eli acted the role, and then Lee—this time minus the butter in his hair—sang the songs.

Lucky for us, Lee has a pretty good voice. And he's a fast learner, Stephanie realized.

Michelle hurried over to Stephanie. She was dressed as an angel for a number in the second act. "It's going great, don't you think?" she whispered.

"Yeah," Stephanie said. "I think it is great. I just hope the audience agrees."

Anna sang the last notes of "Hopelessly Devoted," ending Stephanie and Michelle's first act. The curtain closed.

Instantly a roar went up from the audience. Everyone cheered and clapped and whistled. It sounded as if twice as many people were applauding as there actually were in the auditorium.

"They love it!" Michelle shouted. "And they love Anna and Peace!" She didn't need to be quiet now. Not with all that noise.

Stephanie gave one of Michelle's costume wings a playful tug. "You really are an angel," she told her little sister. "Thank you for saving the show!"

Michelle grinned. "No, thank *you*, Stephanie!"

"Me?" Stephanie asked. "I almost ruined the whole thing."

"No, you were right all along," Michelle said. "Peace is such a good actress! And she's a big star! Having her in the show helped us sell a lot more tickets! Plus, without you, we wouldn't have these great costumes or have been able to use this auditorium."

Stephanie laughed. "And without *your* quick thinking, there wouldn't have been anything to *watch*."

"Everyone's changing into an Act Two costume now," Michelle pointed out. "I'm going to tell them what a great job they're doing."

"Good idea. I'll be right there. I just have to see if Mr. Lang needs anything," Stephanie said. The music teacher was waving to her from the backstage door.

"What's up?" Stephanie asked when she reached him.

"I wanted to know if you and your crew would be willing to do another set of shows next weekend," he said. "Everyone out here has been asking me if there are going to be more performances. But there are no more tickets left for this weekend!"

Stephanie gave a little hop of excitement. "Yes! We can do another set of shows next weekend. That would be so great! We could earn twice as much money for Samantha. Just let me check with the cast."

He nodded. "I better get back to my orchestra," he said. He ducked back out the door.

Stephanie turned toward the dressing rooms and saw Peace watching her.

"I heard," Peace said.

"I know you're probably incredibly busy, but do you think—" Stephanie began.

"Are you kidding?" Peace exclaimed. "This is the most fun I've had in forever. Everyone in my acting class is older than I am. And I get tutored by myself. You guys are my only friends in the whole city."

"I'm glad we got the chance to be friends again," Stephanie said.

"Me, too. And we have to stay in touch, even when I go back to L.A.," Peace answered. "I never know when I'm going to need someone to help me deal with a bully with a jar of paste."

She smiled. "Or give me the straight deal about not belonging in a musical."

"Anytime," Stephanie promised her. "Come on, let's get changed."

She and Peace made their way toward the girls' dressing room. Stephanie opened the door, and Michelle ran up to her. "Steph, look what came for us!" she exclaimed. She thrust a bouquet of tulips into Stephanie's hands.

"They're gorgeous," Stephanie breathed.

"I waited for you to read the card," Michelle said. She carefully opened the thick blue envelope. "It's from Samantha!"

Stephanie leaned close, so they could read the card together. It said:

Dear Michelle and Stephanie,

I don't want to say break a leg, because if you did, you'd end up in the hospital, too! But I will say good luck.
Good luck!
Thanks so much for helping to earn the

money for my operation. I know everyone thinks that Peace Smith is the star of
your show. But to me, you two are the
real stars!

Superstars!

Love,
Samantha

Stephanie swallowed hard. She put an arm
around Michelle. "Samantha's right. You are a
superstar. A superstar sister!"

Michelle threw her arms around Stephanie
and laughed. "So are you, Steph. So are you!"